On the shore were Shells, Shrimps, Crabs, and Starfish. In the water were Birds with long legs, Crocodiles, and Boats. (This Butterfly doesn't belong here. It flew over from the other side.)

Under the water were Coral Insects, Fish, and Sea-Anemones. And there were ever so many more strange Animals and Birds and Insects and Plants and Fish on the Island and in the Sea. But I haven't room in this letter to tell you about them, or about the wonderful and exciting adventures the Dolls had. You will find all these things in the story called.......... Floating Island

FLOATING ISLAND

This Book Belongs to

William, Annabel, and Finny Go under the Waterfall

FLOATING ISLAND

Written and Illustrated by

Anne Parrish

WITH SKETCHES BY MR. DOLL

HARPER & BROTHERS Publishers NEW YORK AND LONDON

FLOATING ISLAND

FLOATING ISLAND

v

CONTENTS

ILLUSTRATIONS

FLOATING ISLAND

Chapter One

CHILDREN, PLEASE HELP ME

Children, I need your help.

Somewhere in the world is a Doll House, with a family of Dolls living in it. Can any of you tell me where?

I can tell you about the Doll House. I can tell you about Mr. and Mrs. Doll, William Doll, Annabel Doll, Baby Doll, Dinah the Cook, and Lobby, Chicky, Finny, and Pudding. I can tell you the strange, exciting things that happened to them, so strange that even I can hardly believe them. But I can't tell you what has become of them.

Can you tell me?

This is their story, as far as I know it.

Chapter Two

ONCE UPON A TIME THERE WAS A DOLL HOUSE

Once upon a time there was a Doll House. It was painted canary yellow, and had a pointed roof, with two surprised-looking chimneys. There was no front to it, so you could look right into the four rooms, each of which had a window with four glass panes.

Downstairs were the parlour and the dining-room. Upstairs were Mr. and Mrs. Doll's room and the nursery.

The parlour was the room Mrs. Doll liked best. There were red rosebuds on the green carpet, and gilt rosebuds on the white wall-paper, and a fireplace that looked as if it were made of chocolate, and had poker and tongs, and a fire of shiny red tinsel. "So much better than a real fire," Mrs. Doll said. "It never goes out, it never smokes, and there aren't any sparks to burn holes in my beautiful carpet."

There was a round table on which was stuck a flower-pot holding a blue bead flower with a yellow center and green leaves. "So much better than a real plant," Mrs. Doll said. "It never fades, and I never have to water it."

There was also a piano, with four white keys and two black ones painted on the keyboard, and a scrap of music

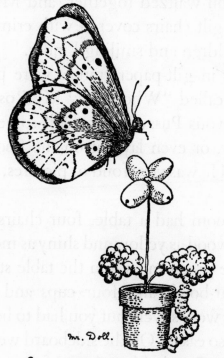

mr. Doll.

Mrs. Doll's Plant. Of course there were no Butterflies and Caterpillars in the Toy Shop. This picture was made later, on Floating Island. The bead flower puzzled all the Insects.

the size of a postage stamp on the music-stand. The name of this was "Waltz of the Dolls." At night, when there were no people in the Toy Shop where the Doll House stood, and the Dolls could move about, instead of staying straight and stiff, Mrs. Doll often played it, while William and Annabel Doll waltzed together, and Mr. Doll sat in one of the four gilt chairs covered with crimson brocade, watching his children and smiling kindly.

Two pictures in gilt-paper frames were pasted on the walls. One was called "Who'll Buy My Roses?" and the other, "Mischievous Pussy." Mr. Doll sometimes leaned against his chair, or even lay flat on the floor, to gaze at these for hours. He was very fond of pictures, and sketched a little himself.

The dining-room had a table, four chairs, and a sideboard, made of wood as yellow and shiny as molasses candy, and a carpet like green moss. On the table stood a teapot, cream-jug, sugar-bowl, and four cups and saucers, that looked as if they were silver; but you had to be careful with them, they bent so easily. On the sideboard were four white cardboard plates. One held a plaster fish with three tiny slices of plaster lemon on him, like yellow buttons on a silver coat; one held a bright red plaster lobster; one held a plaster roast chicken, a beautiful brown, with frills of green paper parsley; and one held a pink plaster pudding decorated with chocolate-coloured squiggles. These were called Finny, Lobby, Chicky, and Pudding, and were friends of the family. The Dolls often pretended to eat them, but they wouldn't really have done so for anything. Mr. and Mrs. Doll liked Chicky best, Annabel and William liked Pudding best, Baby, though still too young to say which was his favorite, was always trying to get hold of Lobby, and Dinah the Cook liked Finny best because nobody else did.

Mrs. Doll had promised Dinah that if ever they could find a really good soap-box they would add it to the house for a kitchen, so Dinah spent much of her time looking out of the dining-room window to see if she could catch sight of a soap-box.

Upstairs in Mr. and Mrs. Doll's room were the bed and two pink chairs, a dressing-table with a muslin frill, and a silver paper mirror with a gilt paper frame.

The nursery had two white beds, one for William and one for Annabel, a crib for Baby, a blue carpet, and two pictures. Annabel's picture was "Cherries Are Ripe," and William's was "The Charge of the Light Brigade."

In the nursery, too, was the most wonderful thing in the Doll House. A tin bathtub, blue outside and white inside, with a tank that would hold a thimbleful of water. Then, if you turned the tap, the water ran into the tub.

The Dolls tried not to boast about their bathtub, but they couldn't help being proud of it.

That was what the Doll House looked like in the beginning, still so new that the paint was sticky.

I wonder, I wonder, what it looks like today!

Chapter Three

THE FAMILY

The Dolls were as different as members of one family often are.

The grown-ups were stiff and could not bend. I mean, they could not bend when people were looking at them. You know how dolls are. I have watched them for hours, and I have never seen a doll move about. But when they are alone, who knows what they do? I suppose that is why we sometimes find them in such strange places. Down behind a sofa pillow, or out in a rain-wet garden. They must have been running about, enjoying themselves, and suddenly known that people were near, and gone straight and stiff again.

Mrs. Doll's hair was fuzzy and yellow; Mr. Doll's was shining black china. He had a black china moustache, and little black china boots, his cheeks were bright pink, and no matter what was happening to him (and, oh, what things did happen, as you are going to hear!) he smiled pleasantly. He was always dressed in evening clothes, and so was Mrs. Doll. His were black and white, and hers were a pink silk ball gown and lace-edged petticoat and drawers.

mr. Doll.

This is
William

THIS IS
ANNABEL

Mrs. Doll never got used to her
children looking straight at
her when their backs were
turned.

William and Annabel Doll could bend all over. Their legs and arms were jointed, and their heads could turn all the way round. Mrs. Doll never got used to her children looking straight at her when their backs were turned. But

Mr. Doll smiled pleasantly and said, "That's what it is to be young!"

William's hair was brown china, and he wore a blue sailor suit.

Mrs. Doll said of Annabel, "The child is exactly like me." For Annabel not only had long yellow hair, but lace-edged petticoat and drawers. She had also a white dress, and a bit of pink ribbon around her waist for a sash.

Baby Doll was pink china, and always stayed in the same position, arms up, with tiny dimpled hands spread out, legs kicking.

Dinah the Cook was jointed, but her head wouldn't turn. She was made of wood, painted black, with big whites to her eyes, and a red mouth as round as a berry. Her dress and her turban were plaid—dark pink, light pink, black, and yellow; her apron and kerchief were white and she wore two blue beads for ear-rings.

Now you know what the Dolls and their House were like on the day when Mrs. Doll was leaning against the piano stool, pretending to play "The Waltz of the Dolls," Annabel Doll was dancing alone, because William Doll wouldn't stop looking at Pudding in the dining-room, Dinah the Cook was gazing out of the window for a really good soap-box, Mr. Doll was having a nap flat on his back on the bedroom rug, and Baby Doll was kicking in the bathtub.

That was the day when Elizabeth's Uncle Henry came into the Toy Shop.

Chapter Four

SETTING SAIL FOR THE TROPICS

Elizabeth's Uncle Henry had come to buy a birthday present for Elizabeth. The minute he saw the Doll House, he said, "Just the thing!" bought it, told the lady in the Toy Shop where to send it, and wrote on a card, "Many Happy Returns of the Day to Elizabeth, with love from Uncle Henry."

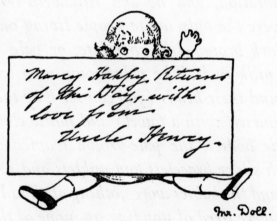

Many Happy Returns of the Day, with love from Uncle Henry.

Mr. Doll.

The Lady in the Toy Shop gave Uncle Henry's card to Annabel to hold.

Then the Dolls and their House were nailed up in a box, and started out, in the dark, on their strange adventures.

Elizabeth lived far away, across the sea, in the tropics, where it is summer the year round. Now I want to tell you something about Elizabeth and where she lived, and yet it doesn't belong in the Doll's story. So I will put a star like this,* and that will mean, please look at the bottom of the page for another star, and read what is written after it.*

* *Elizabeth lived in the tropics, and if you have studied geography you know what "tropics" means, and if you haven't, yet, ask some grown-up. Elizabeth's father owned a cocoa plantation, and he and Elizabeth's mother and Elizabeth were the only white people living on it. All the rest were dark brown, like chocolate, or pale brown, like cocoa with milk in it. The pale-brown men wore turbans twisted around their heads (you can see how they looked if you try it yourself with a towel) and white clothes twisted around their bodies; the pale-brown women wore white clothes, with silver bracelets and anklets and ear-rings and nose-rings; and the babies wore nothing at all but their skins. When they were tired of standing up, none of them ever sat on chairs, or even on the ground, but just squatted wherever they were, as if they were playing Squat Tag. And when they wanted to carry things, they carried them on their*

heads. Elizabeth has seen one person carry on his head a big bunch of yellow bananas; another, on her head a glass of medicine for her baby; another, on his a tray of red and silver fish, just out of the blue sea; another, on hers an enormous basket of cocoa pods; another, on his a spool of cotton; another, on hers a cock and three hens in a hamper; another, on his a hollowed-out bamboo stem, stopped up at the ends, and full of water; and so on and so on and so on.

Try it yourself. Take this book and carry it on your head, without touching it with your hands, while you walk around the room.

Now don't you think those pale-brown people are clever?

The cocoa beans grew in purplish-brown pods, like small ridged footballs, on low trees, and among them stood taller trees called Nurse Trees, because they took such good care of the cocoa trees. By day the Nurse Trees spread their leaves wide and were like giant parasols that kept the hot sun from burning the cocoa trees. But by night the Nurse Trees folded their leaves, letting the dew fall through onto the cocoa trees, to wash them and give them a drink.

The brown-skinned people picked the cocoa pods for Elizabeth's father, and put them on ships, to be carried across the ocean where the beans were made into cocoa and chocolate.

If you are not too busy the next time you are drinking a cup of cocoa, or eating a chocolate, think of the brown people, the Nurse Trees, and Elizabeth.

Now please go upstairs on the next page, and I will tell you what happened to the Dolls.

Chapter Five

STORM AT SEA

Of course the Dolls were in the dark, in their box, and they couldn't imagine what was happening to them, for at one moment they would be right side up, and the next

mr. Doll

The Dolls were in the
Dark.

15

they would be standing on their heads. But they were packed in so well with soft paper and shavings that they stayed in their places. They thought it was night, so they all fell asleep, except Mrs. Doll, who went on playing "The Waltz of the Dolls" even when she and the piano were upside down (of course she made no noise, so she didn't wake anyone) and Dinah, who was watching from the window to see the moon rise.

I must tell you something the Dolls didn't know. They had been put on a ship called *The Pride of the Waves,* that was to carry them across the sea to Elizabeth's nursery.

One night when *The Pride of the Waves* was far out upon the ocean a storm came up. Thunder boomed and roared; the black sky was cracked with blinding white lightning; the waves rose higher than houses, toppled, and fell on the ship, until her sides cracked like a nutshell in a pair of nut-crackers; she trembled all over, and sank, bow first, to the bottom of the sea, leaving nothing to show where she had been except a few things floating—a life-preserver, an apple-barrel, a mast, and, among the rest, the box that held the Doll House.

Now I must tell you something I think you will be glad

to know. You remember what I asked you to do when you
came to a star. Look down.*

Everybody on board The Pride of the Waves *was saved.
They got into lifeboats, with water and ship's biscuit, and
the sailors rowed them all night, up the waves as if they were
climbing mountains, and down the waves as if they were
coasting into valleys. Everyone was frightened, but everyone was brave. The gentlemen and the little boys even said,
afterwards, that they had quite enjoyed the excitement.*

*When the sun rose the storm was over and the sea was
smooth. They had water and biscuit for breakfast (their
night in the open air had given them splendid appetites).
Some apple-barrels from the ship had burst open, and rosy
apples were floating on the blue water, so the children
bobbed for them over the sides of the lifeboats. By noon the
passengers were picked up by another ship,* The Spanish
Lady, *and no one was any the worse for the adventure,
except old Mrs. Robinson, who felt rather tired until she
had a nap (but not too tired to tell the passengers on* The
Spanish Lady *all about the shipwreck), and Mr. Thompson,
who lost his wig. But everyone said he looked nicer without
it, since his head was just like one of the apples, rosy and*

shining, and it had been a bother to keep his wig curled and brushed and combed, so he really didn't mind.

At first it was thought that Topsy, the ship's cat, had been lost. But just as the sailors sadly gave up hope of finding her, she came sailing alongside of The Spanish Lady *in a work-basket belonging to a little girl named Mary. The sun was shining on her black fur, her green eyes gleamed, and she was purring away like a boiling teakettle.*

Everyone cheered, even Mrs. Robinson, and after Topsy had sneezed seventeen times, and had a saucer of milk, she washed herself all over with her rough pink tongue, stretched, yawned, curled up in the sun for a nap, just like Mrs. Robinson, and never felt a bit the worse for her shipwreck.

Some one told me later that she said she was sorry they had rescued her, as she had been looking forward to sailing all the way across the sea in Mary's work-basket. I don't know whether I believe this. I knew Topsy a long time, and I never heard her say a word, although she had her own way of telling you things by purrs and miaous, or even by keeping still. And if she hadn't been picked up by The Spanish Lady, *where would she have found any milk? I asked her that, once, but she walked away with her tail in the air, pretending not to hear.*

As for The Pride of the Waves, *she was an old ship, and found it a pleasant change to rest quietly on the bottom of the sea, after going back and forth across the top of it for so many years.*

She lay, all covered with silver bubbles, among branching trees of white and crimson coral, and groves of sponges that looked as if they were trying to copy the coral, growing in branches, in cups big enough to hold you, or in tall tubes, down which little fish could swim, like swallows flying down chimneys.

The sand drifted through cracks in her sides and piled softly around her, but sometimes a round silver-white moon floated over her head, as it used to float in the sky, and she saw hundreds of stars, just as she used to see them, and would dream she was sailing again.

But the floating moon was a jellyfish, and the swimming stars were purple and orange and sand-coloured starfish.

She was never lonely, for fish came from miles around to see her. Rising and falling, swimming forward, swimming backward, sometimes slowly, sometimes swiftly, they filled the water around her. Some were like a drift of silver leaves; some were round as balloons and prickly as chestnut burrs. Their mouths kept opening and shutting. Perhaps they were telling one another about this strange sight, perhaps they were trying to read the name painted on her bow.

There was never a day when two or three sight-seeing parties didn't swim around her masts, where sea gulls once had flown, or in and out her portholes. The lady fish admired the pretty gardens on her deck, where lilac and orange sea anemones grew, with black sea eggs, sharply bristled as porcupines, and smooth pale purple sea cucumbers, lying among them. The gentlemen fish inspected the boiler-room. And the young fish played Follow-My-Leader in and out of the spokes of the big wheel by which she once was steered.

That is all I have to tell you about The Pride of the Waves *and* The Spanish Lady.

Chapter Six

WRECKED ON THE ROCKS

When their box was flung into the sea, the sleeping Dolls awoke. Mrs. Doll stopped playing the piano, Dinah stopped looking for the moon. Oh, they were frightened! They longed to rush to one another, but they were so tightly packed that no one could stir; each one must stay alone. Mrs. Doll could hear Baby crying in the bathtub, and Mr. Doll shouting "We must all keep calm!" Then came such a screaming* and such crashes and booms** that she could hear nothing else.

The Dolls could feel themselves being thrown high in the air. Then they would fall down

down

down,

and then,

* *This was the wind.*

** *Partly thunder. Partly the ship breaking up.*

bang! they would seem to hit the bottom of everything. Then up and around, whirling and spinning like a top.

Drawn by Mrs. Doll.
This is when we were so
frightened. It is just
the way it looked. This
is the only picture I have
ever made, but it seems
to me quite easy. Mrs. Doll.

"Keep calm! Keep calm!" shouted Mr. Doll, but nobody heard him.

Have you ever awakened at night, when you were alone, and everything was black? Suppose, instead of being able to turn over in bed, or reach for your handkerchief under your pillow, blankets and sheets were packed so tightly around you that you couldn't move even the tip of your finger. And suppose your house suddenly shot up higher than the highest steeple, spun around, shook, swooped to earth, then up to the sky, over and over again, with screaming and whistling and roaring and crashing going on outside. And suppose your mother was packed in her room just as you were in yours, so, no matter how loud you called, she couldn't come to you.

If you can imagine all that, you know how the Dolls were feeling.

This went on, and on, in the black darkness, until at last the box was shot upward and crashed—*boom!*—against something, bursting into splinters and throwing the Doll House in a smother of spray over the rocks and on to the land.

Chapter Seven

DAWN ON THE DESERT ISLAND

Mrs. Doll opened her eyes.

She was lying propped against the ruffled edge of a big pink-lined sea shell, on soft white sand. The sun had not yet risen, but the sky above her was a delicate pink. "Like the inside of the biggest pink china teacup in the world," Mrs. Doll said to herself.

"Hush—hush—" What was that? "Hush—hush—" came from far away, and "Hush-sh-sh" came out of the shell she was leaning against.

She got up stiffly.* In front of her lay the sea. Its green water was stained pink with the sunrise, it moved as gently as if it were breathing in its sleep. Foam-edged ripples slipped over the sand and drew back, whispering, "Hush."

* Mr. and Mrs. Doll were both stiff at first because they weren't sure whether there were people on the beach or not. Besides, they had been packed so long and so tightly they felt as your foot does when it goes to sleep.

24

"Where am I?" said Mrs. Doll. "How did I get here?" and then suddenly cried: "My husband! My children!"

Mr. Doll answered, from where he lay propped against a rock:

"Here I am, my dear. Good morning! Isn't this a beautiful morning?"

"Where are we? What has happened?"

"Do you see that blue thing, my dear?" asked Mr. Doll, pointing to the sea.

"No, I don't. What blue thing?"

"All that blue water." For the pink of the sunrise was fading.

"Oh, you mean all that green water!"

"Blue-green, then. But it looks more blue to me."

"Green as the Doll House carpet!" said Mrs. Doll.

"Well, anyway, that is the Ocean.* Now I will tell you what I feel sure has happened. You remember when we were going up and down and around in the dark?"

"Can I ever forget it?"

* *I am always being surprised by the number of things Mr. Doll knew. The reason for this was that he had read so much. There were many books in the Toy Shop, and at night he used to go out and read them and look at the pic-*

tures. That was how he knew the ocean when he saw it for the first time.

Often William and Annabel, each holding one of his hands, went with him, and, puffing and panting, for the covers were big and heavy for a little doll, he would kindly open the books for them and turn over the pages, while his children took pleasant walks across the pictures. Sometimes they walked on flowery meadows, where William would practise jumping from the pink-edged daisy a caterpillar was using for a parasol, to the white-dotted scarlet toadstool whose fat stem was hollowed to make a home for ladybugs, and Annabel would do tight-rope walking on the clothes-line hung full of tiny drawers, stretched from toadstool to harebell. Sometimes they walked in snow, where a gnome in a pine-cone cap, with icicles hanging from it and from his nose, and a beard of icicles, stood under a mountain-ash tree on whose snow-capped coral berries rose-breasted grosbeaks feasted. Sometimes they walked through a starry sky with little angels flying about. Or, if it was a picture of the sea, they would lie down and pretend to swim.

While they looked at the pictures, Mr. Doll would run back and forth across the opposite pages, reading the stories to them.

Sometimes Mr. Doll Read Aloud from the Toyshop Books

"I believe we were on a ship. And you remember when there was a big—BANG!"

He shouted "BANG!" so loud that Mrs. Doll jumped, pressed her hands above her heart, and cried:

"Please *never* do that again!"

"I'm sorry, my dear! But there *was* a big ——"

"Don't!" gasped Mrs. Doll.

"Bang," whispered Mr. Doll. "And I believe that big —you know what—came from one of the islands that float about on the sea. I believe an island crashed into our ship and wrecked it!"*

"So this is a floating island!" said Mrs. Doll.

"This is Floating Island, my dear. That is its name."

* *Mr. Doll didn't always quite understand the things he found in books. You see, he thought islands floated on the sea, like ships. No one had ever told him that an island usually stays in its own place.*

Yet I have heard of floating islands in the tropics. They are fastened to the river bottoms by the roots of the plants that grow on them; they rise in floods, and fall when the water is low, and sometimes an island, with its plants and animals, will break loose and float on the current, and even be swept out to sea.

"How do you know? I don't see it written anywhere."
"I have named it, just this minute," said Mr. Doll.

mr. Doll

What she saw made Mrs. Doll scream
and fall back.
(I am sorry to say I don't think this is a
very good picture of my beautiful pink silk
ball gown. Mrs. Doll.)

"Oh," said Mrs. Doll.
"And now we must look for the others." Mr. Doll got

up. Then he fell down again and lay gazing at the sky.

He was still smiling pleasantly. But Mrs. Doll saw a crack running through his black china hair. Poor Mr. Doll! He had hit his head upon a rock.

"Oh, my dear! You are cracked!"

"Not badly, I'm sure, my dear."

"Lie still until I get you some water!"

"I've had plenty of water, my dear, thank you just the same."

But Mrs. Doll was certain that a little fresh water was what he needed. Looking around for it, she turned away from the ocean.

And what she saw made her scream and fall backwards!

Chapter Eight

THE CASTAWAYS

"What is it, my dear?" cried Mr. Doll, hurrying to her, although he still felt rather dizzy.

Mrs. Doll could only point, at first. Then she gasped, in a voice faint with terror:

"Snakes!"

Mr. Doll was startled, too. But soon he saw that instead of snakes they were the roots of jungle trees that edged the sand. Dark and silver, they twined together, twisted away through the ferns, or made hollows like mouths open to swallow the Dolls. Mr. and Mrs. Doll looked up at huge tree-trunks streaming out into branches, each branch a hanging garden of air plants, with long dangling roots, and blooms so different from the blue bead flower on her parlour table that Mrs. Doll was not sure whether they were flowers or butterflies or frogs. They were pale green, covered with chocolate-brown blotches and streaks, and they had wide-open mouths.

Those silent open mouths of tree roots and air plants

made Mrs. Doll feel as if they were sucking her into them against her will. She clung to Mr. Doll. He was a comfort to her, even if he was cracked.

There were tufts of ferns along the branches, too. "Like feather dusters," said Mrs. Doll.

Mr. Doll.

The Seaweed Bandage made Mr. Doll feel better.

One tree was like a giant fern, or the biggest feather duster in the world. One with silvery branches was covered with thick smooth leaves bigger than all the carpets in the Doll House, and large cups of clear yellow, with crimson staining the base of each petal, running into the yellow as your water-colour paints do when you put crimson too close to yellow before it is dry. One had leaves that were almost black, and very shiny, with light green veins; and flowers like huge pale purple bells.

And every tree was tied to the next by loops of feathery vine.

Through them the Dolls saw a waterfall, sometimes hidden by green, then flashing out again, pouring from one crystal cascade to another, until it foamed, with a rainbow caught in its spray, into a pool at the bottom, and ran across the sand to the sea.

Mrs. Doll found a tiny lilac shell, pleated like a fan, and so thin that the light shone through it. She filled this with water from the stream, bathed Mr. Doll's head, and bandaged it with a bit of seaweed. Then he felt better.

They looked about. There was the Doll House, lying on its back; there were pieces of furniture strewn over the beach. Here was Lobby* half buried in sand and looking quite pale; there was an armchair upside down. Other things bobbed gently out on the water—the parlour table and the piano.

But nowhere, on sea or shore, was there a sign of William, Annabel, Baby, Dinah, Chicky, Finny, or Pudding.

Do you remember who Lobby was? He was the red plaster Lobster.

Chapter Nine

THE CRAB IN THE BATHTUB

"My children! Where are my children?" shrieked Mrs. Doll, falling backward.

"William! Annabel! Baby!" shouted Mr. Doll, and then, for it seemed unkind to leave her out, "Dinah!"

"My children!"

"Be calm, my dear! *Please* be calm!" Mr. Doll sprinkled some water from the sea-shell over Mrs. Doll, who was wet enough already.

"Will-*yum*! An-na-*bel*! Ba-*bee*! *Di*-nah!"

"Hush—hush—" whispered the waves. "Hush-sh-sh" murmured the sea-shell. And they could hear the rush and splatter of the waterfall. But nothing else.

Mrs. Doll lifted her china hand, and shut her wax eye-lids, *tight*. "Hush!" she said, like the waves and the shells. Then she opened her eyes and smiled peacefully.

"My children are alive and well," she said. "There is something in a mother's heart that always knows."

Mr. Doll wondered if there was something in a father's

heart that always knew. So he tried squeezing his eyes tight shut. Yes! He, too, felt that his children were alive and well, although where they were he hadn't the least idea.

"Is there something in a mother's heart that tells you where we can find them, and when, my dear?" he asked.

Mrs. Doll shut her eyes again. "Wait a minute," she said. "Yes! We shall find them somewhere—sometime!"

Well, that was a relief! Now they could think of other things.

"*Look* at the House!" said Mrs. Doll. "All upside down!"

I told you the House was lying on its back. Mr. and Mrs. Doll looked in through the windows, and saw that each room was a pool of water. Mrs. Doll jumped as a tiny Angel Fish, pale blue, pale green, pale rose, like a bit of the sea at sunrise, swam up to the dining-room window and looked out at her, goggle-eyed with surprise, opening and shutting its mouth.

"I think he's trying to tell us something," she said, and rapped on the window, calling, "Please speak a little louder!"

With a whisk of its tail the Angel Fish turned, and swam through the door into the parlour. Mr. Doll ran around to that window. "I think he was trying to tell us that the fire is still burning under the water!" he called.

Mrs. Doll hurried after him.

"There never was such a fire!" she said. "But, *oh,* what a mess!"

All the wall-paper was soaking and blistered, though Mr. Doll was pleased to see the pictures still sticking to the walls.

"How shall we ever get things tidy again?" asked Mrs. Doll. "It makes me feel quite faint even to think of it!" And she looked as if she were going to fall again.

"Let me get you a chair, my dear," said Mr. Doll, and walked up the beach. Then she heard him exclaim:

"Well—I—never!"

"You never what, my dear? You never what?" cried Mrs. Doll, hurrying to him.

"I never saw such a thing! Look at that, if you please!" Mr. Doll pointed to the bathtub, under a ledge of rock. It was full of sea water, and a very small Crab was taking a bath in it.

"What! Im! *Pert*inence!" gasped Mrs. Doll. "Tell him it's a private bathtub, my dear!"

"Oh, well, he isn't doing any harm," said Mr. Doll, who hated hurting anyone's feelings.

"That isn't the question," said Mrs. Doll. "This is Private Property, No Trespassing. Speak to him, my dear!"

Mr. Doll.

The little Crab tumbled over the side of the tub.

"He couldn't know it was ours," said Mr. Doll, who was thinking that the Crab's claws looked as if they could give a good hard pinch.

"Shall I have to do it myself?" asked Mrs. Doll.

So Mr. Doll, smiling pleasantly, said, "Excuse me, but this is a private bathtub."

The small Crab tumbled over the side and scuttled away without a word. Mr. Doll looked after him and sighed.

"I think we should have been kinder to him," he said. "After all, he might have been able to tell us where we are."

"I thought you said we were on Floating Island."

"I know its name, my dear, but I don't know where it *is*. And suppose this beach is *his* Private Property? Suppose *we* are trespassing?"

But it was too late to think of that now, for the crab had disappeared. The beach was empty, except for sea shells, and silent, except for the hush of the waves.

Chapter Ten

WHAT HAPPENED TO WILLIAM

After the whirling and tossing, the shooting up and the shooting down, that had gone on in the dark, there had come stillness, and William Doll, tired from all the excitement, had gone to sleep.

When he awoke he didn't know where he was. Sunlight was pouring down on him, hot and bright. He was lying in shallow water, that was growing shallower, soaking into the sand with a sucking sound. Soon there was no water at all, only smooth wet sand, with here and there a bubble bursting.

Around him rose a circle of jagged overhanging rocks that looked to William higher than a chimney. How could he ever climb out? He saw no way. "I'm not frightened!" he said, very loud.

The rocks were hung with glass-green seaweed, full of the air balloons that help it to float on the tides. The first thing to do was to burst some of the balloons. *Pop! Pop!* That made William feel better.

Then he looked all about him. Above, high, high above, was the bright blue sky. Below that, the rocks. At the bottom, the sand, with water welling up in his footprints, and here and there a half-buried shell still holding some drops of the sea.

First he tried climbing.

It was hard work, but he got quite far before the ledge of rock began to jut out like the edge of a roof. Then, leaning back to try to catch hold, he slipped on some seaweed, lost his balance, and fell on his back, head first.

It was such a long fall that he had time to imagine his head hitting a rock on the bottom, and cracking like an egg shell.

But the seaweed broke his fall and he landed on the sand, shaken but whole.

He had to lie still for a minute, his joints felt so weak.

Then he tried again, and couldn't get as far as the first time.

"Well," he thought, "I'll just hunt until I find some opening."

There were plenty of openings, for the coral rock was as full of them as a bath sponge is full of holes. But although there were so many entrances,* there weren't any exits.**

*Where you go in.   **Where you come out.

William felt his way through dark passages that twisted about and branched off into other passages, until he was all mixed up, and was thankful to find his way back to the light.

Then he tried shouting.

No answer came except the swish—swish—that must be waves washing against the rocks outside.

Now I will tell you how William got there, and then you'll know more than he did. I'll tell you in a note.***

When William was too tired to scramble and fall and shout any more, he decided to rest and think things over.

*** *The waves flung the box that held the Doll House against the rocks so hard that it flew into pieces as if it were exploding.*

Some of the things in it were tossed onto the beach. You already know what became of the Doll House, Mr. and Mrs. Doll, Lobby, and some of the furniture.

The teapot that looked like silver, being heavy, went slowly down, down, down, among the sponge and coral forests. A little Butterfly Fish saw it, and swam off in a hurry to tell his mother. Back she swam with him, and twenty or thirty of his brothers and sisters, until the

Little Four-Eyes Sees the Doll-House Teapot

blue water was like blue air full of butterfly wings, fluttering in different directions.

That was what Butterfly Fish (and his mother and father and brothers and sisters and uncles and aunts and cousins) looked like—a big butterfly wing, softly shaded light and dark brown and pale yellow. On each side of his body (and the bodies of his mother and father and brothers and sisters and uncles and aunts and cousins) was a white-edged black dot, like another, bigger eye.

Little Four-Eyes and his family lived in a grove of ruffled, branching coral trees that seemed to be covered with delicate purple and orange feathers. But as the teapot fell softly among branches of one, that coral tree turned white. For what looked like feathers were the finely-fringed heads of sea-worms, drawn into their holes in a hurry.

Among the corals grew purple sea-plumes, much taller than you, and huge rosy-purple sea-fans, fine as the finest lace. There were sea-creatures like parasols of waving deep-pink fringe on the tops of pale-pink stems. There were the enormous round corals called brain corals, with big dark sponges growing on them. Little crabs hid among the sponges, and even planted bits of sponge on their rough shells, to help them hide from bigger creatures that might gobble them up if they saw them. And there were other *sponges, with long white tails like spun glass. There were squids that could turn from white to red, and shoot out clouds of darkness by day and of fire by night, to hide in when they were frightened. There were other creatures, strange and lovely. Think of flowers of the softest colours, blue icicles, violet ferns, orange feathers, and the prettiest orna-ments you ever saw on a Christmas tree, all come to life. What is hidden beneath the sea is stranger and lovelier still.*

But the Butterfly Fish were used to all these things, and they thought the teapot that looked like silver was more wonderful than any of them.

They consider it their greatest treasure, and they only use it on grand occasions, like birthday parties. Of course such a large family has many birthdays.

You will think I have forgotten that this note was put in to tell you how William happened to be where he was.

William and Something Else (you will find out what when we go on with the story) were thrown by a wave into the Circle of Rocks.

Annabel
Baby
and Dinah
were ———

But we haven't come to that yet.
This is the end of the note.

He sat down on a shell that was curled like a cinnamon
bun. But he jumped up in a hurry, for out of the shell

William Finds Pudding.

came a pair of wet grey horns that waved slowly, then
drew themselves in.

Of course he wasn't frightened, but he went as far away
as he could from that shell, towards another, pink and

brown, sticking out of the sand. Just as he was going to sit on that—carefully, this time, and looking out for horns—what was his joy to see that it wasn't a shell at all, but his old friend Pudding!*

William took a shell—a flat one, this time, that couldn't hold horns or other surprises—shovelled the sand away from poor old Pudding, and then gave him a hug. It was a comfort not to be alone, although, of course, William had not been really frightened.

"I'll never leave you, Pudding," he said. And, indeed, it didn't look as if he ever could.

With Pudding (who was rather fat and heavy) under his arm, William again hunted for a way out. Then he tried digging an underground passage with his shovel shell, but the passage filled up with water and was more like a well than a tunnel.

Then he shouted, and listened, and heard only the swish of waves outside.

He tried climbing once more, but it was harder, with Pudding under his arm, and the sixth time he fell from

* *This is what I meant when I said William and Something Else were thrown by the wave into the Circle of Rocks. Something Else was another name for Pudding.*

the rocks he was so discouraged he just lay on his back, looking up at the sky.

"Pudding," he said, sadly, "I don't believe we'll ever see Mother and Father and Annabel and Baby and Dinah and Lobby and Chicky and Finny again."

And just then—what was it he saw?

Over the edge of the rocks a sky-blue claw waved against the blue sky, disappeared, appeared again, and then a pair of round black eyes, like shoe-buttons on stalks, looked down at William and Pudding.

Chapter Eleven

WHAT HAPPENED TO DINAH

When the box that held the Doll House burst on the rocks, Dinah the cook was thrown higher than the sky (she said afterwards). She thought it was lucky the sharp points of the stars were all covered with clouds, or she might have caught her skirt on one and hung there for ever. As it was, she fell down again, onto the black glassy slope of a wave that was pouring back from the rocks, and this carried her out to sea.

She had fallen face down, and, as the storm grew less, she saw through the darkness beneath her strange swimming fires. These were the fish that carry their lanterns with them. Some glowed all over, some had little lamps set in their heads, some in their tails, and some in rows down their backs. When it grew light, they vanished, but there were other things for her to look at.

The water was so clear and blue that Dinah felt as if she were floating in the sky. But instead of birds flying beneath her, fish were swimming.

Some were silver, so like her plaster Finny that she felt friendly towards them. But others were so queer that she hardly knew whether they were fish.

There was a Parrot Fish.* He was silver beneath, changing to green, rose, violet, and sea-blue, with a blue-green head, and a tail you could hardly believe. First a touch of yellow, bright as a canary's feathers, then green, like sunlight through leaves, then violet, flame-colour, and violet again. He wore two narrow frills, the one down his back vermilion, and the one where his waistcoat would be, if fish wore waistcoats, dark red edged with blue. His transparent fins were dark blue. He was beautiful, Dinah thought, but his mouth looked so cross that she decided

---

* *Dinah did not know the names of the fish she saw. She could only have told you what they looked like. But I think I had better tell you their real names, when I know what they are myself. Then if you ever meet them you will know them, and be able to call them Angel Fish, Parrot Fish, or whatever they are. The fish may like this better, too. Wouldn't a Parrot Fish rather be called by its own name than just Fish? As you would rather be called by your name than just Girl, or Boy.*

not to say Good-morning. A fish looking like that might snap your head off.

Then came something black as herself, long and slender as a snake, wearing two little black fans on his neck.

Here was something that hadn't the same shape for a minute at a time, for it folded, spread, waved, and looked like jelly turned out of a bowl and come to life.*

Then a School-teacher Fish, with jet scales, like a lady's party dress. Her round face, the fins at her sides, the edge of her dorsal fin** and her tail, were such a bright yellow that if you took the yellow in your paint-box and painted it thick and clear on a piece of white paper, and then looked through it with a light behind it, the School-teacher Fish's yellow would still be brighter.

Then several tiny vermilion fish that Dinah thought must have hurt themselves, for each one had a white bandage around its head. But when she asked them what had happened, they darted away.***

A Jellyfish.

*** Dorsal fin means the fin that runs along the fish's back. Try saying "dorsal fin" to some of the grown-ups. You may surprise them.*

*** Dinah was mistaken, for the white on each fish*

wasn't a bandage, but just a marking. These little vermil-
ion fish have a name almost bigger than themselves. They

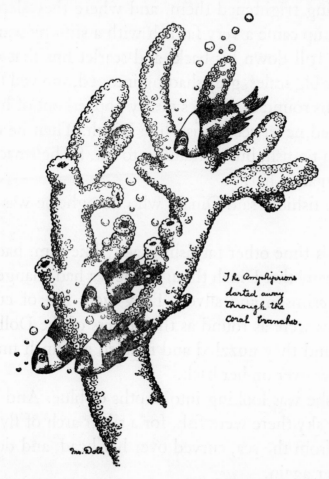

The Amphiprions
darted away
through the
Coral branches.

ms. Doll.

are called Amphiprions. I certainly don't expect you to re-
member that.

When Dinah spoke to them, they hurried back to the garden of apple-green sea anemones where they always hid if anything frightened them, and where they slept.

Then up came a very fat fish with a stumpy scarlet tail, a scarlet frill down his back, and scarlet fins that were so filmy the big scales, grey shading into red, showed through them. His round black eyes nearly popped out of his head, for he had never seen a fish like Dinah. Then he decided she wasn't a fish, but something to eat. So he smacked his mouth against her.

"Nice fishie!" said Dinah, who thought he was kissing her.

By this time other fat fish, exactly like him, had swum up, so many that Dinah thought the sea had changed from blue to crimson and silver. They were full of curiosity, their eyes were as round as the saucers of the Doll House tea-set, and they nuzzled and nibbled at Dinah until they rolled her over on her back.

Still she was looking into depths of blue. And even in the blue sky there were fish, for a silver arch of flying-fish sprang from the sea, curved over her head, and dove into the water again.

There were seagulls, too, flying so high that they looked like a snowstorm, then swooping so low that their breasts were stained green with the quivering reflection of the water.

"Well, it's all very beautiful," thought Dinah. But she would have given all the fish in the sea for a sight of her dear old Finny, with his slices of plaster lemon. Not one of these fish had lemon on it. "What kind of fish do they think they are?" Dinah asked herself. "I never before in all my life saw a fish without slices of lemon on him!"

Rocking gently on the swell, the poor little black doll began to feel terribly frightened and lonely.

"Where are the others?" she wondered. "Shall I ever see them again? Shall I ever see Mr. and Mrs. Doll, William, Annabel, Baby, Lobby, Chicky, and Pudding? Shall I ever see Finny again?"

Chapter Twelve

IS THERE SOMEBODY ELSE ON THE ISLAND?

Now we have left William and Pudding in the Circle of Rocks, with a pair of eyes belonging to we don't know what looking down at them.*

We have left Dinah floating on the sea.

And we haven't found out anything about Annabel, Baby, Chicky, and Finny.

But instead of telling you right away what happened to any of them, I am going to make you wait, and take you back to Mr. and Mrs. Doll on the beach. This is known as suspense.

Sometimes when people know what a word means, they don't like having it explained to them. So if you know what suspense means (I didn't, when I was your age) don't

* *I know what the eyes belonged to, but I'm not going to tell just yet. That comes later in the story.*

read the note at the bottom of the page. If you don't know, the note will explain.**

"The first thing to do," said Mrs. Doll, "is to dry our wet clothes."

So Mr. Doll tugged at a long rootlet until it broke and sent him sprawling. Then he tied it from twig to twig of a bush, for a clothes-line, and on it they hung his black suit with its white shirt-front, Mrs. Doll's pink ball-gown, her lace-edged drawers and petticoat, and her yellow wig, which had come unstuck with all the water. This left a round hole in the top of her head. You could have looked right in and seen the weights that opened and shut her eyes.

"How cool! How comfortable!" cried Mr. Doll, running around in the sunshine and taking a dive (with a good deal of splash) into a pool in the rocks.

*** Suspense means having to wait to know what is going to happen. It is supposed to make you more interested. Suspense can be uncomfortable, like not knowing what your punishment is going to be when you have told them you ate the chocolates you were told not to touch; or it can be splendid, like wondering what is going to be in the toe of your Christmas stocking.*

But Mrs. Doll was hastily getting into a large green leaf. She stuck her arms through it—*ping!*—*pung!*—wrapped it close, and tied a vine tendril around her waist.

"Come here, my dear. I have another leaf for you."

"Oh, do I have to dress?" asked Mr. Doll.

"Of course, my dear! We are new people here, and callers might come at any moment. It's bad enough to have the house upset and to have lost our cook, but how would I feel to have strangers catch you running around without anything on?"

So Mr. Doll sadly got into his leaf. But it wasn't so bad. It was much more comfortable than his evening clothes.

By this time the sun was high in the sky, making the leaves glisten as if they were wet, and the white sand and the waterfall shine so the Dolls could hardly look at them.

"We need sun-helmets, my dear," said Mr. Doll. "I've heard that people in the tropics always wear sun-helmets."

"And I want to keep my head empty," Mrs. Doll replied. "I don't know what I should do if I got something in it."

So Mr. Doll found a bush of small white flowers, like bells, and picked two of them. They made splendid sun-helmets.

"Now we must arrange some place to live," said Mrs. Doll.

"Can't we just camp on the sand? It would be so pleasant! The air is so fresh, and the view is so fine. I could sketch, and you could collect sea-shells. See, here is one, to start your collection! This one coloured and spotted like the Noah's Ark giraffe is a *Terebra subulata*."*

Mrs. Doll did not seem to be paying any attention. She was looking about as if she expected to find another Doll House, right side up, and dry. So Mr. Doll tried again.

"Here is a *Terebra subulata*—I said, a *TEREBRA SUBULATA*—for your collection, my dear!"

"I heard you," said Mrs. Doll. "But this is no time to think of sea-shells. Oh, dear me! Not a house in sight!"

* Mr. Doll had seen a picture of this shell once, and had learned its name by heart. It was the only one he was sure about, so don't be afraid you are going to have such big words to read often.

Wasn't he lucky, to find the one he knew?

It had taken him so long to learn its name, and he was so surprised at having a chance to show how much he knew, that I can't blame him for trying to impress Mrs. Doll, can you?

"Don't you think it would be fun to camp on the sand?"

"I never heard of such a thing in my life!"

"Yes, you have, my dear. You've heard of it this very minute!"

"Well, I never want to hear of it again," said Mrs. Doll. "I want a roof over my head."

"Then how about this cave among the roots?"

"Too damp! The spray from the waterfall reaches it."

"How about a tent of leaves?"

"The wind would blow it down."

"Come and have a look at this coral rock. It's full of little caves."

Mrs. Doll came, feeling doubtful. But it was just the thing! There was quite a big cave* that they could use for a living-room. Over this, easily reached by steps in the rock, were two smaller caves that would do for bedrooms. And around the corner, with a view of the waterfall, was another cave.

"A kitchen for Dinah, at last!" cried Mrs. Doll. "How pleased she will be! If she ever comes back to us," she added, sadly. For while there is something in a mother's heart to tell her the children are alive and well, and will

* *Big for a doll. Small for you.*

return to her some day, there is nothing to tell her whether the cook will come back.

How Mr. and Mrs. Doll did work!

First they cleared all the bits of seaweed and driftwood and shells out of the caves. Then they put down leaf carpets. A big green leaf in the living-room and two smaller blood-red ones in the bedrooms. In the kitchen they left the sand uncovered. "Easier to keep clean," said Mrs. Doll.

The beds were lost, so they made comfortable heaps of springy dry seaweed. Mr. Doll bounced up and down on them. "Excellent springs!" he said.

The living-room was quite grand by the time they finished. Mr. Doll swam out and rescued the piano, which was light because it was hollow, and the round table with the flower-pot. Mrs. Doll let him take off his leaf to do this. They found two of the red brocade chairs. Then, since the tea-set was lost, they chose four flat white shells, tinted with pink, for dishes, and four smaller curled grey ones for cups; and Mrs. Doll set the table with them.

They had found one dining-room chair, and the sideboard, and with these they furnished the kitchen. Oh, how they panted and puffed before they got the sideboard in place! On it they put Lobby, so that he felt quite at home.

And they gathered a small heap of driftwood splinters, ready to light, and some shells to cook in.

Mr. Doll finds a Starfish.

Then Mr. Doll made a discovery. A large powder-blue star by the edge of the ripples! It was too flat for a sofa, and too thick for a rug, so he thought it would do for both. He dragged it to the living-room, and Mrs. Doll said she had never seen anything prettier. But when she stepped on it, it waved one of its points and gave her a terrible turn! So she made Mr. Doll drag it back to where he had found it.*

While Mrs. Doll gathered flower petals for napkins and sheets and towels, Mr. Doll made a path, edged with tiny scallop-shells, that led from their door to the pool beneath the waterfall. Then he found a deep snail-shell to use as a bucket. He was going to fill the bathtub tank with fresh water. They had left the bathtub under the ledge of rock, with two flower-petal towels, and a scrap of real sponge they picked up on the shore. Mrs. Doll wrote, "Private Property, No Trespassing," with a twig, in the sand beside it, and when she was busy in the cave Mr. Doll added: "Unless you want a Bath. If you do, turn the Tap."

Carrying his snail-shell bucket, Mr. Doll walked carefully along the exact center of his path to the pool. "Glug-glug" went the water as it entered the mouth of the shell.

Down drifted a tiny feather, jade green with a fluff of

* This was a Starfish. It was as much surprised as Mrs. Doll.

white, and floated so lightly that it was almost dry when Mr. Doll picked it up. What bird had dropped it? Mr. Doll looked, but in vain. "Would you like your feather back?" he called into the air, but no bird answered. So he stuck it into his sun-helmet, and leaned over the pool to enjoy his reflection.

He liked this so well that he felt gay and dashing. As he carried his water home, brushing his footprints out behind him with a spray of fern, for he wanted to keep his path looking new until all the family had admired it, he sang "The Bluebells of Scotland." That was the tune the Music Box used to play in the Toy Shop, so long ago.

But he stopped singing as Mrs. Doll rushed wildly towards him.

"The clothes-line! The clothes-line!" she cried. "Hurry! A terrible thing has happened! Oh! Oh! Oh!"

Seizing Mr. Doll's hand, she ran with him so fast that the water jumped out of his bucket. She wouldn't even jump on the path. She ran right over the scallop-shell border.

"Please—keep—off—the—grass!" gasped Mr. Doll.

But Mrs. Doll answered:

"Pooh! It's only sand!"

Then she remembered he was slightly cracked, and added, more kindly:

"I'm sorry, my dear. But this has upset me so, I don't know what I'm doing. Just *look!*"

There hung the clothes-line—empty!

There was no wind to have blown the clothes away. There were no footprints in front of the bushes. But Mr. Doll's evening clothes, Mrs. Doll's ball-gown, petticoat, drawers, and wig were gone.

Mr. Doll said, in a voice he tried to make brave:

"There is somebody else on this island!"

Chapter Thirteen

THE SEARCH FOR THE ROBBERS

"There is only one thing to do," said Mrs. Doll.

"Do I have three guesses?" asked Mr. Doll. "Never wear any clothes again!"

"No!"

"Write a note in the sand saying: 'Lost. Some clothes. Please return to Mr. and Mrs. Doll, and receive reward. No questions asked.'?"

"No! Only one more guess."

"Wait and see what happens?"

"No! Now I will tell you. You must hunt until you find the thief, and make him give them back."

"Oh," said Mr. Doll, and added, "But he might be a *lion!*"

"A lion would have left footprints," said Mrs. Doll.

"He might have swept them out," said Mr. Doll, remembering his own fern broom that he used on the path.

"Well, I certainly don't want a lion wearing my wig," said Mrs. Doll. "Now, we mustn't waste any more time.

There's a high hill, that will give a good view of the country. The first thing to do is to climb that and see what you see."

"But I see what I see down here!"

"Not as well as you will up there!"

"But ——"

"And if you see a lion or a humming-bird wearing my wig ——"

"Or my evening clothes ——"

"Or my pink ball-gown ——"

"Or your lace-edged petticoat and drawers ——"

"Just go right up to him, and say ——"

"If he doesn't eat me before I can say anything!" put in Mr. Doll, nervously.

"Perfectly pleasantly," said Mrs. Doll, not paying any attention to what Mr. Doll had said, "I beg your pardon, but I think you have made a mistake. That is my Private Property."

"How about the reward?"

"You can find a pretty shell, and give it to him."

"But whoever took the things could take all the shells he wanted. I think I'd better let him keep my evening clothes."

"Nonsense!" said Mrs. Doll. "Honesty is its own reward."

"How would it do if I drew a little picture and gave it to him?"

"*Suppose He's an Elephant!*"
(*Mr. Doll hopes this looks like a real elephant.*
He has only seen the elephants in the Toy Shop.)

"Well-l-l ——," said Mrs. Doll, doubtfully.

"I tell you! We'll let him take a bath in our bathtub!"

"Suppose he's an elephant!" said Mrs. Doll. "No, no, my dear. Time enough to think of rewards when you find our clothes."

So Mr. Doll toiled slowly up the hill, sliding back in the sand, and thinking he could never reach the top, while Mrs. Doll stood at the bottom and called out things meant to encourage him, such as: "Hurry, my dear!" "Don't slip that way!" "Oop! You fell down, didn't you?" and "Suppose it is a crocodile!"*

But when he reached the top, Mr. Doll stood still, forgetting what he had come for, only happy to be in such a beautiful world. He turned slowly around. Now he was looking at trees whose tops seemed to brush the sky, in patterns more lovely than the ones a kaleidoscope makes. Now he was looking at the waterfall, foaming and leaping, its rainbow arched like a bridge from bank to bank. Now he was looking at the beach, white as snow in the sunlight, with sea gulls walking along it with short rocking steps. Now he was looking at the sea, that spread in changing tints of violet, green, and blue, until it melted into the blue of the sky.

"You were right, my dear!" he called to Mrs. Doll. "The sea is green!"

"What, my dear?" Mrs. Doll called back.

* *The Dolls knew a great deal about animals, for in the Toy Shop they had lived next door to a Noah's Ark.*

"But it's blue, too!"

"I can't hear you!"

"As well as violet. And there is even a little gold!"

"Please speak louder!"

"Never mind! I say, NEVER MIND! I'll tell you when I come down!"

The ocean was edged with white foam, delicate as the lace-paper edge on a valentine, but here and there were frightening streaks of blue, so dark they were almost black. These were made by hidden reefs, where ships could be caught and held until waves pounded them to pieces.

And what was that floating on the water, like a big lilac bubble or half of a lilac balloon?

Chapter Fourteen

THE SEA-GOING CANOE

Mrs. Doll grew impatient, and climbed the hill, too.

"Look, my dear!" Mr. Doll said.

"Where?"

"There, right where I'm pointing. That strange lilac bubble—or is it a ship?"*

"Where?"

"Just under that sea gull—oh no, he's moved."

But Mrs. Doll, although she insisted she was looking right where Mr. Doll was pointing, kept on gazing in

* This was neither a bubble or a balloon or a ship, but the sea animal called Portuguese Man-of-war. It floats on the top of the water. Just under the water comes a big tight bouquet of small bluebell-coloured tubes, and what looks like frills of pale lilac moss, and from this dangle ever so many slender long trailers, white, lilac, blue, and pale green.

It is beautiful, but if you meet one, just look at it, don't try to pat it. Because it stings.

quite another direction. You know how people will do that sometimes, when you try to show them something. And she said:

"A lilac bubble! My dear, I'm afraid you need glasses! It's a pink-and-yellow flower."

"Excuse me, my dear, but if I ever saw a lilac bubble ———"

"With touches of black."

"I can almost see through it."

"Oh no! It is perfectly solid!"

Then Mr. Doll noticed that they were looking in different directions.

"See" cried Mrs. Doll. "Those flying-fish flew right over it!"

Mr. Doll saw what she saw. Black, pink, and yellow. And he cried:

"Why, it isn't a flower at all! It's Dinah!"

"I do believe it is!"

"We must rescue her!"

And he began to pull off his leaf, in order to swim more easily.

"My dear, you can never swim that distance! We'll have to find a boat."

They rolled down the hill in a hurry, and ran along the beach, hunting for a boat.

"Hurrah!" shouted Mr. Doll. "I've found a canoe!"

He came out from under a tree, dragging a fallen seed-pod. It was shaped like a pea-pod, but was bigger and stronger.*

They took out the shiny black seeds, and fitted in a splinter of wood for a seat. Another splinter made a paddle.

Then Mr. Doll took off his leaf defiantly.**

"I'll probably tip over and have to swim," he said.

Mrs. Doll, who had just opened her mouth to tell him to put on a smaller leaf for a bathing-suit, gave a cry and threw her arms around his neck.

"Oh, promise me not to tip over!"

But Mr. Doll wouldn't promise, and he wouldn't let Mrs. Doll come with him. He kissed her good-bye, told her not to expect him until she saw him, ran his canoe down

This was one of the seed-pods called Old Women's Tongues, because of the noise they make when the breezes blow. Clatter, clatter, clatter—as if they were talking together, all at once.

**Defiantly means that he was going to take off his leaf, and keep it off, this time, no matter what Mrs. Doll said.*

the sand and into the ripples, jumped in, and paddled out on the deep.

mr. Doll.

The Pod Canoe.
I meant to draw the whole Ocean in this picture, but it was too big. Mr. Doll

Mrs. Doll, sobbing, but proud of him, watched from the shore. The sea had looked as smooth as a changeable-silk table-cover until the canoe got out on it. Then the gentle swell seemed to poor Mrs. Doll to change to terrible waves. She watched the green feather (for Mr. Doll had kept on his sun-helmet) appear on the top of a wave, the bright drops flash from his paddle. Then out of sight, for so long she thought she should never see him again. Then the tip of the feather—the sun-helmet—Mr. Doll—the canoe, seeming to stand straight up on its end. Then out of sight again.

At last she had looked so hard, and the sun was so bright on the water, that the whole ocean seemed to be covered with tiny bobbing dark canoes, and she couldn't be sure that any of them were real.

Chapter Fifteen

ALONE ON THE DEEP

Being out on the ocean, and looking at it from the shore, are two very different things, as Mr. Doll was finding.

Even the colours were different. No smooth stretch of green and blue and violet. When the canoe shot up a slope towards the sun, that wave was edged with pure gold, and under the gold a narrow line of rose, all warm and glowing. Looking back, Mr. Doll saw that the edge of the wave behind him was silver, underlined with violet, liquid and cool. And in between gold and silver, the hollows were bright dark blue, yet so clear that he could see the grains of sand far below on the bottom.

He was finding the waves very high. Sometimes, from the crest of one, he caught sight of the distant floating speck of pink and black and yellow, and knew he was paddling in the right direction. At other times he could only see tumbling water.

He began to sing, in order to cheer himself up.

"My Dinah lies over the ocean,
My Dinah lies over the sea,
My Dinah lies over the ocean ——"

Something bumped against his canoe so hard that he thought at first it must be another floating island. Then he saw it was a big black-and-yellow fish.

"Please don't push!" he cried. "You nearly knocked me over! Plenty of room for us all!"

But the School-teacher Fish swam along beside him, bumping her face against the canoe, or flipping her tail, so that she nearly swamped it.

Since speaking politely had been of no use, Mr. Doll tried to frighten her.

"When I used to go whaling," he said, very loud, pretending to talk to himself, "I harpooned every whale that came near my ship!"

The School-teacher Fish gave the canoe a harder bump than ever.

"I took my harpoon, and lifted it in the air, this way!" shouted Mr. Doll, lifting his paddle, and nearly falling overboard. "And I threw it like lightning straight into the whale!"

And he poked his splinter of wood at the School-teacher Fish, who didn't mind it at all.

"What shall I do?" thought poor Mr. Doll. *"Shoo! Shoo!* Nice fishie! Swim away, then!"

At this, the School-teacher Fish swam into the green glass hill of a lifting wave, as if to say: "Oh, *that* was what

Mr. Doll.

The Fish Bumps into the
Canoe.
The Fish was really much, much,
much bigger. I hadn't a piece of
paper big enough to draw the Fish as
BIG as she was. Mr. Doll.
P. S. – My sun-helmet blew overboard. Mr. D.

you wanted, was it? Why didn't you say so in the first place?"

Mr. Doll in his canoe shot up to the crest, and found himself staring straight down into Dinah's face.

"Dinah!" he shouted joyfully, and Dinah as joyfully answered:

"Oh, Mr. Doll!"

But just as she put out her hands to catch the paddle he held towards her, down swooped a Sea Gull, caught Dinah in his claws, and flew away with her.

Mr. Doll gazed until they were only a speck—until they melted into the sky.

He had dropped his paddle in his surprise. It had floated away.

Now he was out of sight of land, alone, for even the School-teacher Fish was gone, in a canoe without a paddle.

Chapter Sixteen

THE RESCUE SQUAD

Now where are we?

Mr. Doll is out in his canoe without a paddle.

Mrs. Doll is running up and down the beach, trying to catch sight of him.

Dinah is up in the sky in a Sea Gull's claws.

Lobby is on the sideboard. He is the only one who is feeling peaceful and at home.

Annabel is—where?

Baby is—where?

Chicky is—where?

And Finny is—where?

William and Pudding are in the Circle of Rocks, and have just seen the eyes looking down at them.

"Look, Pudding," William whispered.

But the eyes had gone.

Soon they heard a scrabbling and scraping above them, and then the rocks against the sky were edged with a fringe of waving blue claws.

"Pudding, we are surrounded!" William whispered.

Then one claw came over the edge, feeling its way cautiously, and a little Crab came into sight. He looked quite friendly.*

"Please help us!" William called. "We can't get out!"

The Crab drew back in a hurry, and all the waving claws vanished.

"Come back!" William shouted. *Please!*

Tips of claws appeared again over the rocks.

"Crabs! Ladies and gentlemen!" William began in a hurry. "Pudding and I can't get out, and we don't know what to do! Please help us, and we'll be ever so much obliged. Thank you very much for your kind attention!"

The claws waved as if they were applauding William's speech.

Then they disappeared again.

But they came back, with a long streamer of seaweed,

* *This was the Crab that had been ordered out of the bathtub by Mr. and Mrs. Doll. They had made him feel so badly that when he saw another doll he thought the best thing to do was to run away. But he was kind-hearted. He felt sorry for William and Pudding, and wanted to help them.*

which they let down into the hole. It dangled just out of reach of William's finger tips.

There was only one thing to do. He must push over the biggest shell, the one with the hidden horns, and climb up on it, with Pudding in his arms.

He did it. The horns stayed inside, this time.

William could only use one hand to hold the seaweed, for the other was clutching Pudding.

The Crabs backed away from the opening, pulling the seaweed in their claws.

Up went William and Pudding, spinning around.

Halfway!

Two-thirds of the way!

Almost at the top ——

Snap! The seaweed broke, and *Swish!* William and Pudding were at the bottom again.

But the Crabs had not given up. Down came another seaweed rope, longer and stronger.

William poked a hole with his hand through the damp cardboard of Pudding's plate, pulled a ragged end of seaweed through, and knotted it on the other side.

Up went Pudding, and over the edge of the rocks.

Then the Crabs let the seaweed down again, and William tied an end around his waist. He was lighter now,

without Pudding, and had both hands to hold with, and
they got him up.

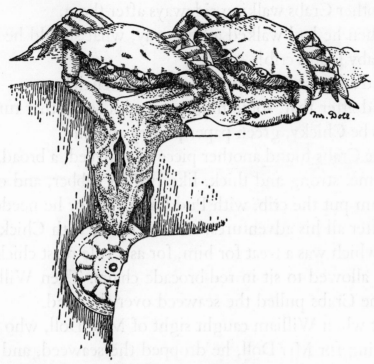

The Crabs Pull Pudding Out of the Hole.

Oh, how happy he was! He jumped up and down, and
hugged Pudding, and tried to say "Thank you" to the
Crabs, who stood around in a pleased circle, shyly scraping
the sand with their claws, blowing bubbles out of the sides
of their mouths, and making sounds like watches ticking.

Then the first little Crab beckoned with his claw, so William, picking up Pudding, followed him along the beach, with other Crabs walking sideways after them.

When he had walked a little way, what should he find but Baby Doll's crib!

And a few steps farther on, a parlour chair!

And after that, something grey with sand, that turned out to be Chicky, green-paper parsley and all!

The Crabs found another piece of seaweed, a broad one this time, strong and thick, like ruffled rubber, and on it William put the crib, with Pudding in it, for he needed a rest after all his adventures, and the chair, with Chicky in that, which was a treat for him, for as a rule roast chickens aren't allowed to sit in red-brocade chairs. Then William and the Crabs pulled the seaweed over the sand.

But when William caught sight of Mrs. Doll, who was watching for Mr. Doll, he dropped the seaweed, and ran as fast as he could, shouting:

"Mother! Mother!"

Oh, they were happy to be together again!

After William had told his mother all his adventures, she turned to thank the Crabs, and invite all of them to use the bathtub as often as they liked. But they had vanished like raindrops falling into the sea.

William was delighted with everything—the Doll House full of water, and the little Angel Fish, who was now looking in astonishment at the picture of "Mischievous Pussy"—the new coral cottage—the shell-edged path to the pool.

Mrs. Doll got him out of his damp sailor-suit, and spread it to dry in the kitchen. No more clothes-lines for her, thank you!

Then William behaved just like his father, and didn't want to wear anything. But she dressed him in a leaf and picked him a sun-helmet.

"Where are the others?" asked William, who thought perhaps they had gone on a picnic or a lion-hunt. He didn't want to miss anything.

"Your father is out on the ocean in a canoe. He has gone to rescue Dinah, who is floating about beyond her depth."

"And where are Annabel and Baby?"

But Mrs. Doll could only answer:

"Oh, where?"

Chapter Seventeen

TWO WISHES COME TRUE

You remember the Sea Gull snatched Dinah into the air just as she was going to catch the paddle Mr. Doll held out to her.

Up they went until Mr. Doll and his canoe looked as small as the period at the end of this sentence. Up they went until Dinah could see, under the water, the round hollow islands the coral insects build, and the big dark patches of floating seaweed.

Dinah saw something else floating, and what do you think it was?

A really good soap-box!

I told you how she had looked and longed for one, to turn into a kitchen. And here was the best soap-box you could imagine! It was floating with a few other things from the wreck of *The Pride of the Waves*. It was clean and new and strong, just what Dinah had always wanted. And there she was, up in the sky with a Sea Gull. She couldn't possibly reach it. She just had to watch it bobbing on the waves.

"I shall never see such a beautiful soap-box again!" she
said, sadly.

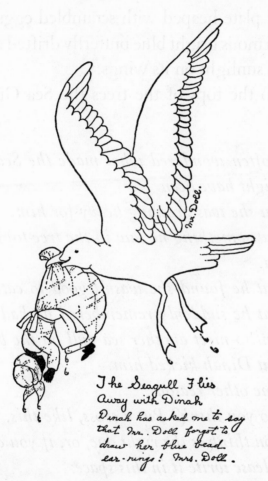

The Seagull Flies
Away with Dinah
Dinah has asked me to say
that Mr. Doll forgot to
draw her blue bead
ear-rings! Mrs. Doll.

Wasn't that hard luck?
Then the Sea Gull flew inland, and the sea of blue water

beneath them turned into a sea of green leaves. Here and there she saw a tree so full of yellow blossoms that it looked like a round plate heaped with scrambled eggs. Here and there an enormous bright blue butterfly drifted and slanted, catching the sunlight on its wings.

Then into the tops of the trees the Sea Gull dropped Dinah.*

I have often wondered what made the Sea Gull drop Dinah. It might have been

    1. That she was growing heavy for him.

    2. That something he saw in the tree-tops frightened him.

    3. That he found she wasn't good to eat, after all.

    4. That he suddenly remembered he had an engagement to meet another sea gull on the beach.

    5. That Dinah kicked him.

    6. Some other reason.

Which do you think? Put a cross, like this, X, opposite the reason you think is the right one, or, if you can think of one better, please write it in this space:

    7.

Dinah fell through the leaves ——

Swish ——

      sh ——

           sh ——

                sh ——

                     sh ——

and landed head first in a soft tuft of ferns springing out of the crotch of a bough.

She picked herself up and looked around. She was on a bough that was as broad to the little doll as a wide road would be to you. Most of it was so covered with moss and tiny ferns that it was as soft beneath her feet as velvet cushions stuffed with down. She took a walk along it, and followed some of the branches that led out like narrow paths through the leaves.

Looking down over the edge, she could only see other leaves and branches, so thick that there wasn't a glimpse of the ground.

Looking up, she saw the same thing; not a glimpse of the sky.

"I don't care," she said to herself. "I've had enough of the sky for one while."

No one was in sight but an insect walking along the central vein of a big leaf as a traveller would walk along a road. Dinah spoke to him, but he paid no attention.

"Such airs!" said Dinah. "Proud of your green-and-gold suit, aren't you? You wait till you see my lady's pink ball-gown and yellow wig! You won't think you're so wonderful then!"

She might as well make herself comfortable, for here she was, and here she would have to stay, as far as she could see, until Mr. Doll managed to find her. "If he found me out in the middle of the ocean, he'll find me up in a tree," she thought.

First she would dry her clothes, sticky with salt water. She spread her apron, kerchief, turban, and dress on the branch, but kept on her blue bead ear-rings.

The tree she was in had blossomed in showers of trumpets, looking so much like the trumpets in a brass band that Dinah expected them to burst into music.

As she stood looking up at them, one of these slipped from its stem and fell right on top of her, covering her head, as a candle-snuffer covers a candle.

Dinah pulled it off.

I have always been sorry she never knew how she looked at that moment. I'll tell you why.

There were two things Dinah had wished for more than anything else in the world.

The first was to catch sight of a really good soap-box.

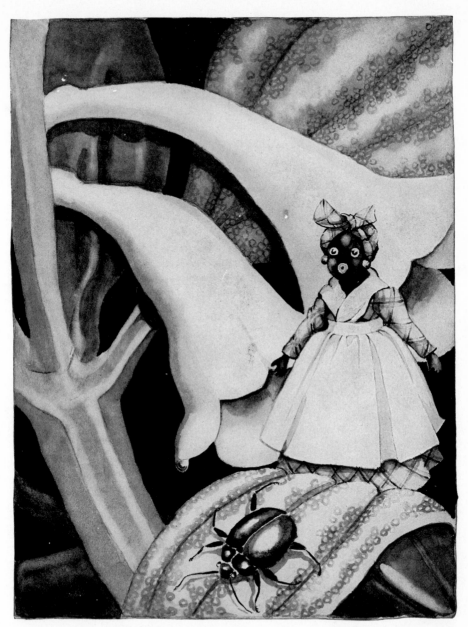

The Insect Is Too Proud to Answer Dinah

We know she had just had that wish, and much good it did her!

The second was to have yellow hair like Mrs. Doll's.

And as she pulled her head out of the trumpet flower, her black wool was golden-yellow with pollen.

She couldn't see herself, and of course there was no one to tell her.

In one hour Dinah's two greatest wishes had come true, and the first did her no good, and the second she never knew about.

But the flower gave her an idea. She put it on again, and pulled it down until her head stuck through the top. It made her a beautiful skirt.

Then she sat down in a loop of vine, gave a little run and a push. Up flew her swing, and back, higher and higher. Oh, what fun!

She began to feel light—bubbling—what was it, exactly? Happy! That was it! Although she was lost and alone, she had never been so happy, and although she had never been here before, she felt more at home than she ever had felt in her life.

As she swung, she began to sing:

"Rockabye, Dinah, in the tree-top,
    When the wind blows, the cradle will rock ——"

Then a strange thing happened!

Chapter Eighteen

IN THE TREE-TOPS

Dinah had noticed, when she was strolling up and down the bough, that no breeze was blowing. She would certainly have felt the slightest one, with nothing on but her earrings.

Yet, although most of the leaves were still, one here and there moved slightly.

Now, as she sang, these leaves left their branches and came crowding about her. And she saw they were not leaves, but little lizards, green on their backs, cream-coloured underneath. Some clung to the bough with all four feet, some sat up on their tails and hind legs, with their front legs bent. And out of their throats swelled big semi-transparent * orange bubbles.

"Well—I—never!" Dinah exclaimed, and then:
"Oh, my *land*!"

* *Semi-transparent means that you could almost see through them, but not quite.*

For a still stranger thing had happened. One of the lizards darted from the moss to a bare patch of tree-trunk,

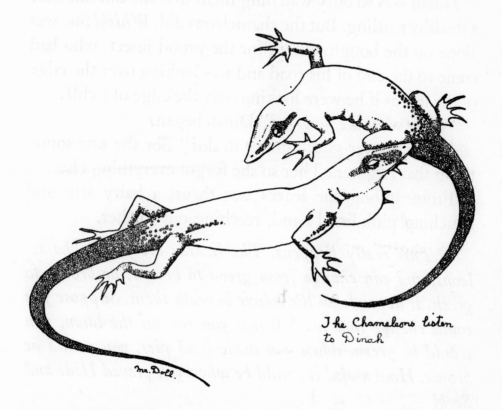

The Chameleons listen to Dinah

m. Doll.

and while Dinah watched him he turned slowly from green to brown.

She didn't believe her eyes. But another followed, and the same thing happened.

Then the first went back to the moss, and turned slowly from brown back to green.*

Dinah was so busy watching them that she did not hear a stealthy rustling. But the chameleons did. *Whisk!* She was alone on the bough, except for the proud insect, who had come to the end of his road and was looking over the edge of the leaf as if he were looking over the edge of a cliff.

"*Now* what are you —?" Dinah began.

But she never said, "going to do?" For she saw something that frightened her so she forgot everything else.

From among the leaves was thrust a hairy arm and clutching pink-lined hand, reaching out for her.

* This really happens. The lizards are called chameleons, and can change from green to brown, or brown to green. It depends on the colour beneath them. Suppose you could change that way! When you ran on the lawn, you would be green, when you made mud pies, you would be brown. How useful it would be when you played Hide and Seek!

Chapter Nineteen

WELCOME TO THE HERO!

"When will Father be back from his canoe trip?" William Doll asked his mother.

"He should have returned long ago," Mrs. Doll replied. "Run up that hill and see if he is coming."

William climbed the hill, and saw Mr. Doll paddling his canoe, quite near the shore.*

William didn't stop to run down the hill. He rolled.

"Father's coming! Father's coming!"

"Run and get a bouquet to greet him with!" cried Mrs. Doll. "Oh dear, I wish I had time to put up an arch with 'Welcome' done in flowers!"

She did the best she could. She seized a twig and wrote

WELCOME TO OUR HERO

Perhaps you think I have forgotten that Mr. Doll lost his paddle. But he pulled out the driftwood-splinter seat and used that for a paddle.

in big letters in the sand, while William ran up, dragging a fragrant cream-coloured flower like a cup, bigger than himself, with four little blue-green beetles sitting in it, surprised, but enjoying the ride.

Mr. Doll's canoe came over the crest of a ripple. When he caught sight of Mrs. Doll and William, he began to sing.

"I'm delighted to see *you*,
    Mrs. Doll, my dear, and William!
I crossed the ocean blue,
    Mrs. Doll, my dear, and William!
In my beautiful canoe,
And I thought that I was through,
But away a seagull flew
    With our Dinah!"

Then he stood up, waved his paddle, and shouted, "Chorus!"

"Up the waves and over the waves and under the waves and
    through,
In spite of the swishes of tails of the fishes, we'll paddle our
    pod canoe!"
"I left you in the cave,
    Mrs. Doll, my dear, not William,
And I was brave as brave,
    Mrs. Doll, my dear, and William;
Though I had a narrow shave
Yet I crossed the ocean wave,
But, alas, I could not save
    Poor old Dinah!"

"Chorus!" he shouted. "All join in!"

So Mrs. Doll and William, on the shore, and Mr. Doll, standing up in the canoe and beating time with his paddle, sang together:

"Up the waves and over the waves and under the waves and
　　through,
In spite of the swishes of tails of the fishes, we'll paddle our
　　pod canoe!"

And as Mr. Doll sang "canoe!" he marked time so hard that the canoe turned over and in he went!

William couldn't stand that, so in *he* went. For what do clothes matter when you can gather them on every bush?

After a splendid splash, they came out, and the three Dolls joined hands and danced on the beach until they all fell down.

When William had presented his bouquet, and Mr. Doll had admired Mrs. Doll's Welcome in the sand, each told his adventures.

When the stories were ended,

"Listen!" said Mrs. Doll. "What is that?"

They listened, and heard a bubbling noise. William ran behind a rock, and came back hand in claw with the little Crab.

"This is my friend," he said.

"Why, I do believe it is the gentleman who was our first caller!" said Mr. Doll. "You remember, my dear? In the bathtub?"

"Yes, my dear," said Mrs. Doll, looking ashamed of herself.

The Three Dolls Danced on the Sand.

"Delighted to see you again, sir," said Mr. Doll, with a bow. "Sluvly day!"

"*Don't* say sluvly, my dear!" begged Mrs. Doll. "Say, It is lovely. E-nun-ci-ate dis-tinct-ly!"

"You must stay and have supper with us," said Mr. Doll.

"Yes, do!" added Mrs. Doll. "If you don't mind pot

luck. You see, we have lost our cook, and the House is all upset. In fact, we have only a caretaker in it at present."

"A caretaker, my dear?" asked Mr. Doll, and then remembered the Angel Fish swimming from room to room and trying to tell them things through the windows. So he added: "Oh, yes! But if you would care to go through our House, sir, we could boost you over the side, and our caretaker would be delighted to show you round. You might enjoy seeing our collection of pictures. 'Mischievous Pussy' is especially beautiful."

" 'Who'll Buy My Roses?' is even finer," put in Mrs. Doll.

" 'The Charge of the Light Brigade' is the best of all!" cried William; and then, because Annabel wasn't there to speak for her favourite, he added, " 'Cherries Are Ripe' is all right if you like it."

But the little Crab was tugging at William's hand with one claw, and pointing with the other.

"He doesn't seem interested in pictures," said Mr. Doll, disappointedly.

"He wants us to come somewhere," William explained.

Chapter Twenty

THE ASCENT OF THE ROCKS

The Crab hurried ahead, scuttling sideways, and the three Dolls followed. He led them to some rocks that jutted up sharply.

They were steep, and Mrs. Doll was sure she could never climb them, although Crab ran ahead, flopped back on the sand, and then did it all over again, to show how easy it was. Yet she was unwilling to wait below.

So Mr. Doll ran to the edge of the beach, where the trees grew, and pulled another long rootlet like the one he had used for a clothes-line, and also broke off three twigs. With the rootlet he roped Mrs. Doll, William, and himself together.

"Just like Alpine climbers," he explained.

Then, with their twigs in their hands, for alpenstocks, they began the ascent of the rocks, the Crab leading the way.

Now this island was a coral island, and of course the rocks that stuck up from the sand were coral, too. You know there

is a difference in rocks. Some are hard, and some are softer.
Coral is softer. So, as the years go by, the waves nibble into
it as mice nibble into cheese. The rocks the Dolls were
climbing had been nibbled away, year after year, by the
waves, until they were full of peaks and spires, sharp as
knives and needles, with pools between, where each tide
left some water; sometimes a few drops, sometimes a cup-
ful.

Even you would have a bad time if you tried to climb on
them barefoot. You would be badly cut, and, unless you
were careful, a sea-water pool would catch your foot and
trip you.

If it would be as hard as that for you, think what it was
for the Dolls!

Often one or the other of them would have fallen if they
hadn't been roped together. Sometimes Mr. Doll would
be clinging with legs and arms to one pinnacle, William to
another, and Mrs. Doll would be dangling between them,
as if she, like her dress, had been hung on a clothes-line to
dry. When this happened, she shut her eyes and screamed.
And when they had to jump over the teacup-sized lakes,
she shut her eyes, too.

Most of the time when she wasn't screaming or jumping, she was saying:

"Why did we come?"
Or:
"Where are we going?"
Or:

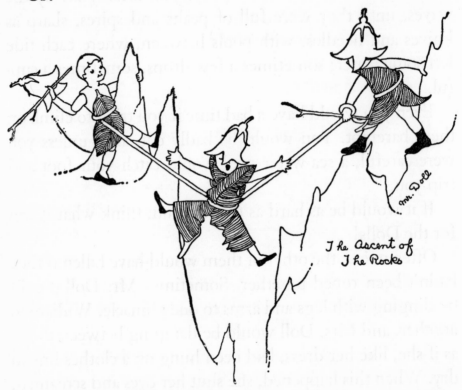

The Ascent of
The Rocks

"How do we know where this Crab is taking us? What do we know about him? He was very kind to William, but what else do we know? Nothing! He may be kidnapping us! He may be leading us straight to the Robbers' Den!"

Or:

"I *can't* jump this!"

Or:

"I *can't* climb that!"

Or:

"I wish we had never come!"

Or:

"Let's go down!"

Or:

"My dear, be careful! William, be careful! Oh, be careful, be careful!"

Or all of them together.

Mr. Doll and William said nothing, because they had no breath left for talking, since Mr. Doll was pulling Mrs. Doll, and William was pushing her. Besides, they didn't know the answers to her questions.

It looked harder to climb down than to climb up, so they kept on.

What you could have done in four big steps was a long hard pull for the Dolls. They had to stop often, and while they rested, Mr. Doll would catch his breath enough to point out the beauty of the view and wish he had brought a sketch-book, Mrs. Doll would ask again why they had ever come, and William would send fragments of rock hurtling down to the sand below, or lean over edges so far that he made Mrs. Doll feel dizzy.

But at last, following Crab, they reached the top, found themselves beside a bigger pool than any they had seen on the way up, and lay down beside it, exhausted.

"A mountain lake!" said Mr. Doll.

"It is only a pool of sea water," said Mrs. Doll. "Why did the Crab bring us all this way just to see a pool of sea water?"

"He's brought us for some good reason," said Mr. Doll. "Just wait!"

"Look!" cried William. "Look!"

Chapter Twenty-One

IN THE OLD CRAB'S POOL

Small Crab had flopped into the water and was walking across the bottom, high on the tips of his claws, raising a cloud of white sand.

The three Dolls lay flat on the edge, watching him.

The water was so clear that looking down through it was like looking through air, except that the shells on the bottom were shaking a little. There was a starfish. "Now, how did *he* get up here?" asked Mrs. Doll, for she thought it was the same one she had stepped on. There was a sea-urchin, prickly as a chestnut burr. On the rocks beneath the water peach-pink and lilac sea-anemones, like thick-stalked, many-petalled living flowers, stirred gently.

At the other end of the pool an old Crab sat on a heap of seaweed, pretending not to notice them. He looked very innocent and absent-minded, sitting there slowly blowing small bubbles from his mouth, as if he had been boiled and still was simmering.

But Mrs. Doll whispered to Mr. Doll:

"That Crab has his eye on us!"

"He looks very pleasant," Mr. Doll whispered back.

"You'll see, he's concealing something, I'm certain!" Mrs. Doll hissed into his ear, tickling it dreadfully.

The little Crab had nearly reached the big Crab. Now big Crab looked at him and raised a threatening claw. Quick as a flash, little Crab darted at the heap of seaweed, gave it a twitch, and scuttled away, big Crab after him.

What was that the little Crab had uncovered?

A white sleeve, a tiny pink outspread hand.

"My Baby!" shrieked Mrs. Doll, and dove into the water.

Mr. Doll and William could hardly believe their eyes. For she had never cared for bathing, except in the bathtub. And she had always been so particular about their going in; they must put on their bathing-suits; they must keep near the shore; they must come out almost before they were in.

Now she was kicking through the water, not caring at all that it was getting into her head (she had lost her sun-helmet on the climb), tearing off her leaf dress when it got in her way, and alarming the sea-anemones so that they folded up and kept perfectly still.

Leaving behind her a wake of ripples and kicked-up

sand, she reached the seaweed, and gathered Baby into her
arms.

Mr. Doll

The Sea-Anemones draw back in alarm as
Mrs. Doll rushes through the Pool.

Mr. Doll and William plunged in, too, and held on to
the big Crab to keep him from catching the little Crab, who

had scrambled up on the rocks and was waving his claw and bubbling away like anything.

"Is Baby—Whoa!—Hold tight, William! Is Baby all right?"

"Not a crack!" Mrs. Doll answered, rocking Baby back and forth in her arms as she sat on the seaweed.

"Then I forgive you for hiding my child!" said Mr. Doll, dropping the big Crab's leg. William still held on, and was dragged halfway across the pool. That was fun!

"Let go, William!" Mr. Doll called. "I'm going to make a speech."

Wrapping a bit of seaweed around him, like a cape, Mr. Doll climbed out on the rocks and made a bow to the Crabs.

"Crabs! Gentlemen! It gives me great pleasure to express to you the heartfelt gratitude of Mrs. Doll, my son William Doll, my Baby, and myself, for your kindness. You, sir"—he bowed to little Crab, who lifted his claw shyly and half turned away—"have returned good for evil, for after having been asked to leave our bathtub, which I hope you will now look on as your own Private Property ——"

"Hear! Hear!" cried Mrs. Doll.

"You first rescued our son, William, and our old friend, Pudding ——"

"Hear! Hear!" cried William.

"And then led us to our Baby. You, sir"—he bowed to old Crab—"took under your care a helpless babe cast up by the sea, who is now restored unharmed to his mother's arms. Knowing our Baby, we realize what a sorrow it will be to you to part from him. Therefore we hope you will consider yourself a friend of the family, and come to see Baby whenever you like."

"Hear! Hear!" cried Mrs. Doll and William, and the two Crabs waved their claws.

"A toast to our friends the Crabs! A toast!" cried Mr. Doll.

"A hot buttered toast, with strawberry jam!" William added.

The two Crabs bubbled their thanks.

"I am reminded of a story," Mr. Doll continued. But here Mrs. Doll called:

"My dear, we should be getting home!"

"I haven't finished, my dear!"

"But you've said everything you needed to say."

"I know, but I've just begun my speech!"

"We really must start for home."

"Very well, my dear," sighed Mr. Doll. He was disappointed. He had meant to make them a lovely long speech, and maybe sing them the song about Dinah.

Because they were now all friends, the old Crab showed them his secret passage through the rocks, so they didn't have that hard climb down.

And I might as well tell you that he came to see them every day. He really did love Baby.

Chapter Twenty-Two

WILLIAM TO THE RESCUE

When Mr. and Mrs. Doll and William and Baby reached Coral Cottage (which was the name Mrs. Doll had given their new home, and Mr. Doll had promised to print in shells on the sand in front) they were all tired.

But there was work to be done before they could rest. First, Baby must be put in his crib. So Pudding was lifted out and allowed to sit in a chair, like Chicky, although Mrs. Doll explained to them that this was a special treat and they mustn't expect to be allowed to sit in the best red chairs every day.

Then the Angel Fish caretaker must be given his supper. William was allowed to do this. He built a stairway of sand and shells up the outside of the House, and climbed it with an armful of seaweed. All sorts of things that angel fish like to eat were sticking to the olive-green ruffles.

Mrs. Doll tried to remember what one should tell caretakers to do. Take care of the fire? No, she could see through the window that the fire was taking care of itself.

Lock the door? There wasn't any door to lock. She couldn't think of a thing. She had to content herself with calling to William:

"Tell the caretaker to take care!"

Then Mr. and Mrs. Doll and William gathered around the table, and had shell plates and shell cups of air for supper.

"Another cup of this delicious air, if you please, my dear," said Mr. Doll, passing his shell to Mrs. Doll.

"But, my dear, you've had two already. I'm afraid you won't sleep a wink!"

However, she poured him another shellful.

"When do we start?" asked William.

"Don't speak with your mouth full, my son."

William swallowed the air.

"When do we start?"

"Do you know, my dear, I think we ought to do something for those Crabs? . . . Use your napkin, William. . . . We might have them to dinner, with a little music afterwards. I could play 'The Waltz of the Dolls.' I wonder if they dance."

"When do we start?"

"Don't interrupt Mother, dear."

"But ——"

"I might sing them my song about Dinah," Mr. Doll suggested. "Or draw them each a little picture."

"But ——"

"Don't interrupt Father, dear."

"But ——"

"Well, I'm sure we're all ready for bed, after our day of adventures!"

"But, Mother! Father!"

"What *is* it, William?"

"When do we start to find Annabel?"

"The first thing tomorrow, when we are all fresh and rested."

"But we *can't* go to bed and let Annabel be lost all night!"

"Now, William, Mother and Father are just as anxious to find Annabel as you are. But we are all very tired, and it will be dark almost at once. We could do nothing but get lost ourselves if we started out tonight. Tomorrow we will get the old Crab to take care of Baby, pack our lunch, and start out to find Annabel."

"But we *can't* let Annabel ——"

"Something tells Mother that Annabel is safe and well, and tomorrow at sunrise we will start out to find her."

"*But* ——*!*"

"William! Mother knows best! Now say good night nicely to Father and Mother, and remember to brush your teeth."

So they all went to bed.

William could not get to sleep, for thinking of Annabel alone in the dark.

But William could not sleep, for thinking of Annabel alone in the dark.

He got up quietly and tiptoed down the rock. He was going to find Annabel himself.

He thought for a moment of taking Pudding for company. But Pudding looked so fat and pink and peaceful,

asleep in the parlour chair, that William didn't wake him.
He left a message written in the sand:

DEAR MOTHER AND FATHER,
　I hope you are well.　I have gone to find Annabel.
Very truly yours, with lots of love,
Your loving son
WILLIAM.

P. S.—Don't worry.

(I must tell you that Mr. and Mrs. Doll never got William's message, for a wave washed it out in the night.)

Chapter Twenty-Three

INTO THE JUNGLE

"Which way shall I start?" William wondered.

Then he saw a lantern bobbing among the trees, and decided to go part way with whoever was carrying it.

He ran to the bank, climbed up by the roots, and hurried after the lantern.

It led him up and along beside the waterfall. The moon had not yet risen, and except for the lantern, that sometimes disappeared behind a leaf, then bobbed out again, William might as well have been playing Blind Man's Buff. But the sound of the waterfall guided him, and he followed along beside it.

Oof!

He tripped and fell.

Scrambling up, he looked around for the lantern. There it was. But there was another—another—three—four—hundreds!

"My goodness!" said William.

Then a light sat on a leaf beside him, and he saw that it and the rest were fireflies.

"What shall I follow now?" William asked aloud.

"Follow me."

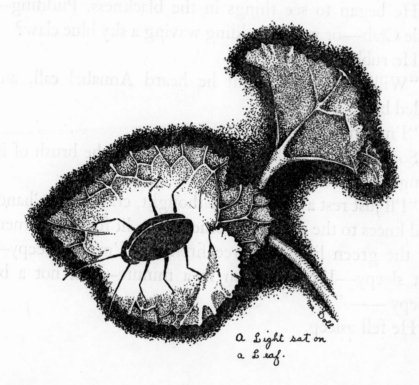

a Light sat on a Leaf.

What was that? Had he imagined the words? For now what had seemed a voice was only the sound of the River.

"Will you lead me to Annabel?" he asked, and listened in vain for an answer.

But surely the River had spoken to him before. He would follow it.

"River, lead me to Annabel!" he cried, and hurried on in the dark, tripping, and falling, and getting up again.

He began to see things in the blackness. Pudding— little Crab—or was it Pudding waving a sky-blue claw?

He rubbed his eyes.

"William!" he thought he heard Annabel call, and called back:

"I'm coming!"

Something flew through the dark, and the brush of its wings knocked him down.

"I'll just rest a minute," he thought, crawling on hands and knees to the shelter of some leaves, lit for the moment by the green light of three fireflies. "I'm not sleepy— not sleepy—I'm going on in a minute—I'm not a bit sleepy ——"

He fell asleep.

Chapter Twenty-Four

SNAIL TRAIL

When morning came, William woke up.

"Where am I? What am I doing?"

Then he remembered. He was on his way to Annabel.

In the dark he had crawled into something that looked like a cave, and had fallen asleep with soft springy leaves between him and the ground. Now, as he moved, the leaves danced under him, and suddenly his foot went through, and dangled in air.

He caught a stem and pulled himself up. Then, cautiously, he looked through the hole he had made.

There is a vine in the tropics that grows twenty feet in a night. William had gone to sleep on it when it was close to the ground, and through the dark hours it had flung out tendrils, clung to branches as tightly as a baby clings to your finger, and lifted itself, growing higher and higher, and carrying William up in a close-woven hammock of stems and leaves.

There he was, in a green cave through which sunlight

poured as if the heart-shaped leaves were green glass, printed with dark patterns of leaf-veins.

He glanced down, and saw that his legs were pale green. They looked as they had when he was paddling in sea water.

He tried to scrub off the green, and saw that his arms and his hands were green, too!

"Oh dear!" he thought. "If I stay green, Annabel won't know me, when I find her!"

He pulled a leaf and scrubbed hard. But the leaf juice only stained him greener.*

At last he gave up trying to get pink again, and looked around for the way out.

"How shall I ever get down?" he wondered, walking as carefully as you would walk on thin ice, to the door of his leafy room, and holding himself up by a tendril above him.

He was a prisoner. Across the opening hung a net. The silken wheel of a perfect cobweb, sagging a little, and blowing in and out with each breath of air, in a broad shallow

*You and I know it was the light falling through the leaves that made William look green, just as the light through a stained-glass window will turn you purple, or crimson, or blue, when it falls on you.

cone. The part in shadow was invisible, but where the light caught it the cobweb shone like silver and bronze-coloured crystal. William touched it, and it trembled all over, but it was strong and sticky, and did not tear.

Since the front door was shut, he would take another look down through the trap-door in the floor of leaves.

The vine had followed the branch of a tree that hung over the River. Far below was a waterfall that would seem small to you, but was enormous to the little doll. The River was stained amber-brown by roots and dead leaves. Bubbles and clots of foam drifted on it, slowly at first, then beginning to race, until they were swept into a pleated crystal fan edged with foam, that spilled over a broad sloping rock.

"That's not a good place to jump into," William said to himself.

He looked once more through the spider web.

The spider who had spun it was resting in a tent it had made by fastening two leaves together with cobweb. It was almost as big as William, with a pink-and-yellow body coloured like a peach, and black-and-white striped legs.

When William tried to get through, he made the web shake and disturbed the spider, who thought a fly must have been caught. So it hurried down for breakfast, dropping almost on top of him.

He was so startled that he jumped back, fell through the hole in the leaves, whizzed through the air, and, *Splash!* fell into the waterfall.

He was swept along, now his head out, now one foot, now all under, from one tumble of water to another, snatching at twigs and leaves, and at last being whirled into an eddy near the bank, where he spun until he was dizzy.

Below him he could hear the loud roar that must be the final leap of the water to the sea, the waterfall near Coral Cottage.

Frantically he caught at an overhanging fern, dragged it down to him, and, hand over hand like a sailor climbing the rigging of a ship, pulled himself to shore.

He was almost back where he had started.

"Well, anyway," William said to himself, "I've come down from the vine and I've escaped from the spider! That's *some*thing!"

And he wasn't green any more. His wet legs and arms were pink. That was something, too.

"Thank you," William said to the River, for he thought it had washed off the green.

What was the River answering?

"Follow me."

Yes, he was sure of it, just as he had been last night, though now the words were lost again in the sound of the water.

He started once more.

This time he could see where he was going, and he had plenty of company.

A leaf-green lizard blew out its throat in a yellow bubble.*

"Good morning," said William. "Do you know where Annabel is?"

But the lizard only blinked.

Two little parakeets, leaf-green, too, sat close together on a branch.

"Good morning," said William. "Do you know where Annabel is?"

But they only kissed each other.

Then he saw a big leaf-green parrot.

"Everyone's green in this jungle," he thought. "No wonder I began to turn!"

The parrot had a yellow head, and yellow-and-flame-

* *This kind of lizard stays green. It is not like the chameleons Dinah saw.*

coloured shoulders. Her beak was curved into a pleasant expression, as if she were smiling.

"Good morning," said William. "Do you know where Annabel is?"

The parrot put her head on one side. Two white lids slid together, one up, one down, over her bright round eye, and she scratched her beak with her claw. But she said not a word.

William has always thought she knew and wouldn't tell.

Then he came to a snail, almost as big as himself. It already had its wet-looking, sand-coloured horns, dark-tipped, sticking out of its curled grey shell, so it didn't startle him. He startled it when he said: "Good morning!" The horns drew in.

"Please, can you tell me where Annabel is?"

Out came the horns, with two shorter ones under them, waved, drew in, appeared again. Then the snail began to pour itself out of its shell. It was wet, pebbled pale tan, with a flattish ruffle of itself on each side. The head lifted until it reared high from the front of the shell, stretching and waving. Then it went down, and the back part came out, too. Now the snail, flat and long, with its shell sticking up in the middle of its back, began to crawl slowly forward, leaving a glistening track of slime.

"It knows where Annabel is!" William thought, walking beside it, and having hard work to catch down with it. You know what it is to catch up with some one who is going too fast. Catching down is what you have to do when some one is going too slow.

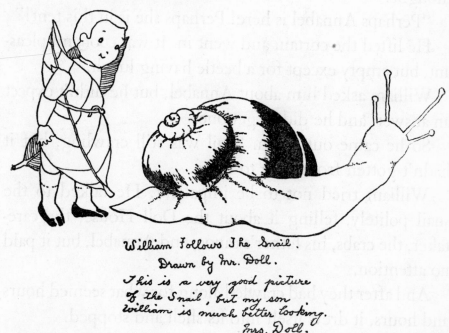

William Follows The Snail.
Drawn by Mr. Doll.
This is a very good picture
of the Snail, but my son
William is much better looking.
Mrs. Doll.

The snail was so slow and its shell was so grey that William thought it must be a grown-up—a very old grown-up, and therefore very wise.

It would lead him straight to Annabel.

But it didn't lead him straight. Every leaf and twig made

it waver and turn, every clump of pink and bronze baby ferns, every fallen seed-pod.

It took so long to get around a big ivory-white toadstool with a web-like curtain dropping from its rim, that William thought:

"Perhaps Annabel is here! Perhaps she is in this tent!"

He lifted the curtain and went in. It was cool and pleasant, but empty except for a beetle having lunch.

William asked him about Annabel, but he didn't expect an answer, and he didn't get one.

So he came out again. Snail was still crawling, but it hadn't gotten from here to there.

William tried not to be impatient. He talked to the snail politely, telling it about the Doll House, the caretaker, the crabs, his father's canoe, and Annabel, but it paid no attention.

And after they had crawled along for what seemed hours and hours, it drew itself into its shell and stopped.

William knew how fond grown-ups are of naps, so he sat down and waited.

And waited ——

And waited ——

And waited ——

And at last the snail poured itself out again, and started back the way it had come.

All of a sudden William decided it didn't know anything about Annabel.

He should have believed the River when it said, "Follow me."

Now the River, and Annabel, and he, were all lost, and night was coming.

Chapter Twenty-Five

THE WRONG RIVER

William was careful about choosing a place in which to wait for daylight.

Night before last he went to sleep, and woke down in the Circle of Rocks.

Last night he went to sleep, and woke up in the air.

Tonight he crept into a sweet white trumpet flower. While he dreamed, the petals drew in, closing over the little Doll, as gently as your mother tucks the sheet around you when you have kicked it out at the bottom of the bed in your sleep. All through the night the flower held him safe, and with morning opened its petals and let in the light.

"Now," said William, when he had thanked the flower, stepped out, and washed his face in dew, "I must find the River again."

He listened for a sound of running water. Far away and faint he thought he heard it, and turned in that direction, pushing through a forest of ferns, and getting a good many shower baths.

It is never very bright in the jungle. The trees make a thick roof, the sunlight can only filter through. The air is hot and steamy as a greenhouse, or a bathroom with the door shut and the tub full of hot water. And when morning turns to noon everything grows silent. Birds and beasts are hidden, resting in the heat of the day.

A twig crackling under his feet sounded so loud that he jumped. But he pushed on, through ferns that held him as if they were trying to say, "Stay with us!" through dew-spangled cobwebs that clung to him and trailed after him. If you had seen him, you would have thought he had covered himself with mosquito netting.

He jumped again as he came suddenly on something white. Long arms, twisting and curving, seemed to reach out to wrap themselves around him.

"I'm not afraid of you!" William shouted; and then felt rather silly when he saw it was a flower. From a long throat came six short round petals, six long slender ones, and six others, longer, like threads.*

"Pooh!" said William. "You're only a flower! You try to scare me again, and I'll—I'll—*pick* you!"

* *The flower was a Spider Lily. It looks like a big white spider with very thin long legs.*

He pushed on, walked for a long time, and stopped with a jump.

Only another Spider Lily. But he hadn't expected it.

He just gave it a look, and went on.

Here was another!

By this time something about it made him wonder. Had he seen three Spider Lilies, or one?

He tied a bit of his trailing cobweb around the Lily's stem, and started out again.

After awhile, another gleam of white.

A Spider Lily. And with a cobweb sash.

Then William knew he was walking in a circle, as his father had told him people sometimes do when they are lost in the woods.

"No good doing *that*," said William. "I could walk in a circle a million billion years and never find Annabel. Don't you get in my way again!" he added, severely, to the Spider Lily, which just stuck out a petal at him, as if it were sticking out its tongue.

How could he find where he was?

A tree stood near, covered with creeping vines, scarlet-stemmed and velvet-leaved, plastered in pretty patterns so flat to the tree-trunk that it looked as if it were trimmed with fancy braid. The boughs, like those of all the other

trees, were loaded with ferns and orchids, and lianas*
dangled down like ropes from the bells in a steeple.

William caught hold of one, and went up hand over
hand.

When he was high in the air he saw something that
made him shout for joy. A flash of flowing white, that
must be the River, with another waterfall pouring into it.

He slid down and ran to it.

But when he came close he saw the river was not of
water. It was made of thousands of ants, and it was running
in two directions.

The stream that showed white was made of ants, each
carrying a tiny piece of flower petal, and through this, in
the opposite direction, a black stream flowed, made of ants
carrying nothing, but going back for fresh burdens. The
double stream ran along the ground, and up and down a
tall tree full of white flowers, until it was hidden by leaves
and branches.**

*A liana is a creeping plant that grows in the jungle,
tying the trees together, and hanging down from them.*

**These ants are called Parasol Ants, because they carry
their bits of leaf or petal like parasols. Another name for
them is Leaf-cutting Ants. They bite out bits of leaves in*

curious shapes, and take them down into rooms dug under-
ground. Other ants are waiting there, whose work it is to

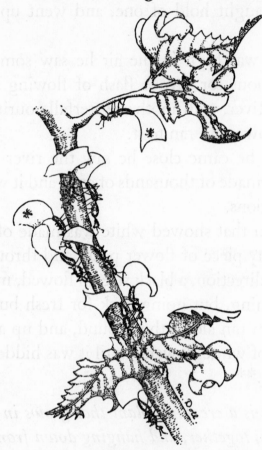

The Parasol Ants.

roll the leaves and petals into balls and plant them with
spore that will grow into tiny mushrooms, to feed the ants
and their babies.

William was so disappointed that if he had not been a boy doll he would have cried.

At the same time, he was interested. The pieces of petal were so much bigger than the little ants, bright and black as wet ink. Here and there he saw a tiny ant sitting on a petal, stealing a ride home to the nest.

He watched the stream of ants so long that, when he looked up, the trees and the ferns seemed to be sliding past, too.

Then he discovered that other ants had cut rooms in the roots of another tree, and had thrown up a heap of sawdust bigger than the Doll House.*

William asked them ever so many questions, but the ants were too busy to pay any attention to him. So he said: "I'm busy myself! I'm much too busy to watch you any more. I'm looking for Annabel!"

He started off again.

* These are the Carpenters, who make nurseries for the baby ants, and mushroom cellars.

Chapter Twenty-Six

DANGER!

Evening was near. A breath of freshness stole through the jungle, and birds and animals began to stir. The frogs sounded like little bells ringing, the crickets cried. But no one had anything to tell William.

A sound of loud sawing over his head made him look up.

There sat a toucan with short stumpy body, all black except for a bib of lemon-yellow feathers, and a huge green banana-shaped beak, red at the tip, as if he had dipped it into a jam-pot.

He looked friendly, but he had no answer for William's question.

Blue butterflies, bigger than William, drifted before him, closed their wings, lined with the colour of dead leaves, then spread them again.

Macaws and parrots, scarlet, green, yellow, and blue, whistled and screamed, but never answered him.

Night came, and with it a sudden terrifying sound, a

loud grating croak. A shapeless mass flopped down from
the dark, almost on top of him.*

mr. Doll.

The Toucan looked friendly, but did not answer.

William ran, as fast and as hard as he could. I hope you

* *This was a Croaking Lizard.*

won't think him a coward. I don't mind telling you that I should have run, myself, if that had happened to me.

He came out in a clearing bright with moonlight. And there he saw something that at first made him feel all his troubles were over.

A crab.

Yet he paused a moment, he hardly knew why. What was a crab doing so far from the sea?*

And this crab was so different from small Crab and old Crab. He was much bigger, and he looked fiercer. The moon made the clearing almost as light as day, and large fireflies darted above him, showing his bright dark purple shell, and his legs shading from purple to vermilion. His two huge front claws were yellow and looked like saw-toothed shears. No bubbles simmered from his mouth. Somehow he didn't look pleasant.

Yet all the crabs William had met had been friendly. Even the old Crab that hid Baby was now a friend. Surely this one would help him.

He waved, rather timidly, and the crab waved back in so welcoming a way that William felt happy again, and ran to him, gasping:

* *This was a Land Crab.*

"Oh, *Crab,* I'm glad to see you! I've had such a time! I followed a lantern and it wasn't one, and then I woke up in the top of a tree and got shut up by a cobweb and fell into the River and nearly went over the waterfall and followed a snail and got lost and got scared, well, not really scared, by a flower, and walked around in a circle and thought I'd found the River but it was only some ants and then something croaked and flopped and I don't know where I am, and *please* will you help me find Annabel?"*

The crab seemed to clasp his claws in sympathy, his eyes

* *If you want to know how William really spoke to the Crab, you must say it all in one word, like this:*

"*Ohcrabimsogladtoseeyouivehadsuchatimeifolloweda-lanternanditwasntoneandtheniwokeupinthetopofatreeand-gotshutupbyacobwebandfellintotheriverandnearlywentover-thewaterfallandfollowedasnailandgotlostandgotscaredwell-notreallyscaredbyaflowerandwalkedroundinacircleand-thoughtidfoundtheriverbutitwasonlysomeantsandthensome-thingcroakedandfloppedandidontknowwhereiamandplease-willyouhelpmefindannabel?*"

Can you get all the way through without catching your breath? William did. You see, he was so relieved to be able to tell his troubles to some one he thought was friendly.

popped with surprise and interest. And when William said, *"Please,* will you help me find Annabel?" he pointed, and then held out his claw. William took it. Hand in claw, they went along together.

Suddenly that bad crab dropped William's hand, opened a cruel claw like a pair of scissors, snapped it around William's waist, and dragged him down a deep black hole.

Chapter Twenty-Seven

THE START FROM CORAL COTTAGE

Every now and then I must stop and see just where we are.

William is down in the Land Crab's hole, with the Land Crab sitting on top of him to keep him a prisoner.

We haven't found Annabel yet.

The last time we saw Dinah, she was up in a tree, and Something was reaching through the leaves towards her.

We haven't found Finny, but Chicky and Pudding we left in the parlour chairs, and Lobby was on the sideboard.

Baby was in his crib.

Mr. and Mrs. Doll were asleep in Coral Cottage.

The morning after William ran away to find Annabel, Mrs. Doll went to wake him, and found his seaweed bed empty.

"Oh, my dear!" she called to Mr. Doll. "Come upstairs at once! More trouble!"

Mr. Doll hurried to her.

"William has disappeared!"

"Perhaps he's taking an early-morning swim."

So they ran out on the beach and looked everywhere, but there was not a sign of William. I told you a wave came up in the night and washed out the message he left.

The little Crab was sitting near the bathtub, looking as if he wanted to get into it, but wasn't quite brave enough.

"Have you seen William?" Mr. and Mrs. Doll asked him together, and then Mr. Doll remembered his manners, and added:

"Good morning! Sluvly day!"

"Not sluvly! It—is—lovely!" Mrs. Doll murmured. But she didn't really care, she was so worried about William.

But small Crab only tucked his claws closer to him. It was clear that he hadn't seen William.

"I believe my brave son has gone alone to find his sister," said Mrs. Doll.

"I'm sure you're right, my dear! That's just what my brave son would do!"

"But we must find him. We must find both of my children. Do you suppose my son has started out by land, or by sea?"

"I think my son has gone by land," said Mr. Doll. "Because the canoe is drawn up on the sand. Why, that's poetry!

"The pod canoe is on the sand,
So William must have gone by land!"

"Then let us go into the jungle," said Mrs. Doll.

Just then old Crab came slowly up, pretending he was out for a morning stroll. He must have known it was too early to pay a call, but I think he was hoping the Dolls would see him and ask him in.

Mrs. Doll carried Baby out, and put him down to kick in the sun.

"Will you two gentlemen please keep an eye on my Baby while we are gone?" she asked.

"Will you please keep four eyes on my Baby?" Mr. Doll added.

"And pinch anyone who comes near him?" Mrs. Doll said.

The Crabs bubbled politely, and settled down to watch Baby.

Mr. Doll thought of making them a little speech of thanks, but Mrs. Doll said there was no time to waste.

"You give the caretaker his breakfast, and enough for lunch, while I make some air sandwiches to take with us," Mrs. Doll said.

So Mr. Doll put a whole stack of seaweed in the water of the Doll House dining-room, with enough breakfasts

and lunches and suppers hidden in its frills to last the caretaker for several days.

"Sluvly day!" he said, leaning so far over the dining-
room wall that he nearly fell in.

"Would you rather have chicken air or ham air in the
sandwiches?" called Mrs. Doll.

"Chicken *and* ham!" Mr. Doll answered, hurrying to
the kitchen cave to see whether any buttery crusts were
left over. He was very fond of them.

"I think I won't take a gun, my dear," he said, leaning
against the sideboard with his mouth full.

"You haven't a gun."

"I know, so I won't take it. But shouldn't I take a paint-
box and pad?"

"No," said Mrs. Doll. "And we shouldn't take any
more time, either."

So they put on their sun-helmets, because that made
them feel more like real explorers, and crossed the beach.

"Ha!" said Mr. Doll. "Hist!"

"What, my dear?"

"A footprint!"

For of course the wave that had erased William's message, as you might erase a pencil mark with a rubber, had
not gone far enough to wash out all his footprints.

"Only one?"

"Only one to begin with. Then another and another and

Mr. Doll's head appeared among the rattling pointed leaves.

another! See, they lead straight to these roots, that make a
perfect ladder up to this cocoanut palm that leans out over

the beach. William must have gone either into the jungle or to the top of this palm tree."

"Just run up to the green feather-duster ———"

"Palm leaves, my dear!"

"And see if William is there, before we go into the jungle."

So Mr. Doll climbed the palm tree. It was a long, hard climb, but the silver-grey trunk had grooves running around it, in which he could just catch hold with his hands and his china boots.

He disappeared among the rattling pointed leaves. Then out came his head.

"A beautiful view from here! Well worth the climb!"

"Is William there?"

"I can't hear you! The leaves make such a clatter. Would you care for a really good cocoanut? There's a beauty here."

"*Is William there?*"

"I can't hear you! I'll be down in a minute!"

He was. His foot slipped, he went on his back, and whizzed down, bumping over the bulges, as if the trunk was buttered. He had to jump to the beach, where Mrs. Doll was waiting, to pick up his sun-helmet.

"Oh, I forgot to tell you William wasn't there."

So they climbed the root ladder, to go into the jungle.

Chapter Twenty-Eight

THE EXPLORERS

"Upsy-daisy!" cried Mr. Doll, boosting Mrs. Doll from behind.

"Now which way? There aren't any more footsteps to follow."

"Here is a broken fern. That is called a clew, my dear."

"Here is a red berry with a bite out of it. Is that called a clew, too?"

Mr. Doll had a look at it. It wasn't a strawberry or a raspberry or a currant, or any berry whose name he knew, so he decided it must be called a clew.

But that was the end of the clews.

"Now what shall we follow?" Mrs. Doll asked.

"We must follow our noses."

"But my nose points in so many different directions."

"Then we must follow mine."

So they followed Mr. Doll's nose for a long way, only stopping now and then to listen, or to pick up his sun-helmet, which was continually being brushed off by some overhanging spray of fern or flower. Mrs. Doll had tied hers on with a veil of twisted cobweb.

Now, will you please do something? Imagine yourself smaller and smaller, until you are just as long as your mother's hand. Then you will be able to guess what the world looked like to Mr. and Mrs. Doll.

The next time you are in the woods, or the garden, put your head close to the ground and see how the crossing stems of grass, ferns, and flowers change to thick forests.

When the Dolls were in the fern forests, they couldn't see the trees at all.

When they came out to cleared spaces, there were other ferns, tiny ones, with as many different shapes as snow crystals have, circles and stars and wheels; and trails and rosettes of leaves, in every shade of green from almost white to almost black. These ran along the roots and far up the trunks of the trees, like breaking waves, only they broke in leaves instead of spray.

Sometimes the Dolls tried to climb over roots that weren't roots at all, but big snakes that glided away. Once they leaned to rest on a rock, and it stuck out a head and four leathery feet, and was a tortoise.

"I don't like these woods!" said Mrs. Doll. "They walk around so!"

"Suppose we stop and have lunch," Mr. Doll suggested. "Then we'll feel better."

"Lunch!" said Mrs. Doll. "My dear! What can you be thinking of?"

"Lunch!" said Mr. Doll. "I'm thinking of lunch! Ham-and-chicken sandwiches!"

"It isn't time for lunch. It still is early morning."

So they struggled on. The way grew harder. Sometimes they had to lean backward with only toe-holds and finger-tip-holds, to get around a rock over a deep pool. Sometimes their feet went through leaf-mould that looked like solid earth.

"This island doesn't like us!" gasped Mrs. Doll. "It trips us up, and shoots out from under our feet, and slips us into pools, and puts big rocks in our way!"

Once they were caught in a blizzard of butterflies. So many butterflies whirled around them that they might as well have been lost in a snowstorm, only I never heard of a yellow snowstorm. Did you? They could see nothing but beating, soaring, spreading, folding wings.

"Put your head down and push on!" shouted Mr. Doll.

When they came out from it they were sprinkled with the gold dust of butterflies' wings.

Sometime, when your head is close to the ground, be

Mr. Doll.

The Blizzard of Butterflies.

P. S.— Take my advice and <u>never</u> draw more than one
butterfly at a time. Your very tired friend, Mr. Doll.
P. P. S.— But there were ever so many more butterflies
than this! Mrs. Doll.

still, and listen to all the faint rustlings and snappings and sighings that go on among the roots.

The Dolls could hear all that you hear, and more. An insect climbing a fern stem; a shower of tiny seeds bursting from their pod and scattering to the ground; the beat of a moth's wings. Mrs. Doll said she could hear the toadstools pushing up from underground, softly and steadily. Perhaps she could, for such tiny ears can hear things we never have heard at all. We carry our heads too high.

But you can hear and see and smell more than the grown-ups can, for you are nearer the many lovely and little sights and sounds and scents that cling close to the earth.

Chapter Twenty-Nine

TIGER, TIGER!

The light in the jungle is dim and green, but sometimes the sun falls through holes among the leaves, and streaks the tree-trunks with splashes of yellow sunshine and dark shadow. The Dolls came to four tall trees, striped yellow and black in this way. Two close together, then, quite a distance off, two more.

"A beautiful grove, my dear!" called Mrs. Doll to Mr. Doll, who had gone between the first two. "It casts such a refreshing shade! Just the place to have lunch!"

But Mr. Doll jumped back right on to Mrs. Doll's china toes, for he had come around a leaf—*Bump!*—into a big black-and-gold insect that glared at him with bunches of bright black eyes, like two blackberries, that could see not only in front, but up, down, to the sides, and behind.

"Whew!" said Mr. Doll, fanning himself with his sun-helmet. "I thought it was a tiger!"

"A tiger!" cried Mrs. Doll. "Really, my dear, if I didn't

know a tiger when I saw one, after living so near Noah's
Ark in the Toy Shop, I'd be ashamed of myself!"

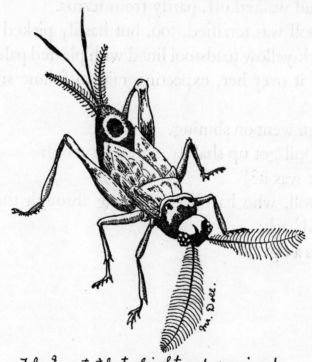

The Insect that ~~frightened~~ surprised
Mr. Doll.

And she leaned against one of the four trees to see
whether Mr. Doll had chipped her china toes when he
jumped on them.

The tree walked away!

All four trees walked away!

And a roar echoed and rolled through the jungle.

Mrs. Doll fell flat, partly because what she had leaned against had walked off, partly from terror.

Mr. Doll was terrified, too, but hastily picked a small, waxy, dark-yellow toadstool lined with pleated pale yellow, and held it over her, expecting rain to follow such loud thunder.

The sun went on shining.

Mrs. Doll got up shakily, and whispered:

"What was it?"

Mr. Doll, who had been peeping through the leaves, whispered back:

"It was a tiger!"

Chapter Thirty

PUSHING ON

They went on more carefully after that, and Mrs. Doll kept jumping, and clutching Mr. Doll's arm, and thinking she heard the tiger.

Mr. Doll said: "Pooh, pooh, my dear! Do you think I'd let a tiger hurt you?"

But he kept looking behind him, and picked a twig the length of your little finger, to fight the tiger with if it should come after them.

They went on under trees that held out arms laden with gifts of ferns and orchids, touched the Dolls, and stroked them with big five-fingered leaves, like cool kind hands.

Mrs. Doll liked the leaves, but she didn't like the orchids.

"They are sticking out their tongues and making faces at us," she complained. "Speak to them, my dear!"

Some of the trees were covered with vines and airplants, hugging them so tightly that they had not been able to breathe, and had died, and turned into hollow wooden lace-work, all beautifully green outside with leaves not their own.

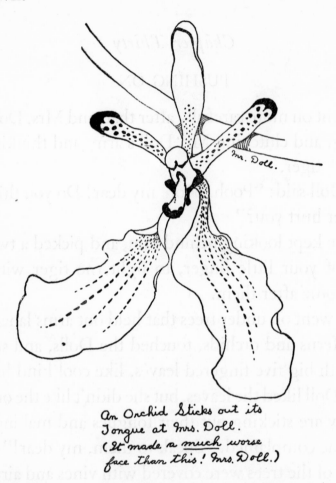

An Orchid Sticks out its
Tongue at Mrs. Doll.
(It made a *much* worse
face than this! Mrs. Doll.)

The Dolls went inside one to rest, and, looking up through the hollow tree, saw the blue sky above them.

"Just like a chimney!" said Mr. Doll.

"Funny chimney, with a hole in it!" Mrs. Doll objected. For she was used to the Doll House chimneys, solid pieces of wood glued to the roof.

There was a steamy smell of mould, wet earth, and rotting wood; and once a flood of sweetness as a tiny humming-bird, green as a leaf with the sun behind it, quivered as if it were caught in a net of air before a white trumpet-flower, darted deep into its throat, and flashed away, leaving the flower shaking.

The jungle was so still it seemed to be holding its breath. There was no sound but the flowing of many little streams, each the width of your hand, and shallow as a pane of glass, that fell over small stones into tiny waterfalls. As they waded the streams, the china boots of the Dolls clink-clinked against the pebbles.

They toiled on, climbing up and down, slipping into hidden pools as deep as teacups. Mr. Doll felt so tired and discouraged, he began to sing to cheer himself up:

"Mr. and Mrs. Doll are we,
Taking a walk through the ferns, you see!
Mr. and Mrs. Doll House Doll
With a beautiful toadstool parasol,
Dressed in leaves, and cobweb string ——"

"Cobweb string, indeed! Cobweb *veil!*" said Mrs. Doll.

"It looks more like a string now, my dear," said Mr. Doll. "Besides, I have to say string to rhyme with the next line."

"You could find plenty of rhymes for veil. Say we haven't caught sight of a single whale, or that seeing a tiger made you turn pale."

"Excuse me, my dear, but I like my own poem better.

> "Dressed in leaves, and a cobweb string,
> And powdered with dust from a butterfly's wing.
> And every step that we take, we look
> For Annabel, William, and Dinah the Cook.
> The forest is large, and we are small,
> But Mr. Doll never is frightened at all——"

"Tiger!" said Mrs. Doll.

"Where?" cried Mr. Doll, jumping.

"You were frightened of the tiger."

"Well—not frightened, only careful. But, to please you, my dear, I'll change that line.

> "The forest is large, and we aren't big,
> But we'll hunt till we find the yellow wig,
> We'll hunt till we find our Annabel,
> And William, and Dinah the Cook as well.
> If we haven't found them extremely soon
> We'll have to hunt by the bright white moon.
> But Mr. Doll (and that means me)

Is a wonderful hunter, all agree.
Mr. Doll isn't afraid of a bee,
Or a flea,
Not he!
He would simply put them over his knee
And give them a smacking, and let them go free.
For Mr. Doll went out on the sea
In a pod canoe,
And what did he do
When he fought with a whale?
He did not turn pale!"

"I told you there were plenty of rhymes for veil," said
Mrs. Doll.

Mr. Doll bowed politely, and went on:

"He told it to go, and it just turned tail
And swam away through a big green wave,
For Mr. Doll is terribly brave ——"

"Tiger!" said Mrs. Doll.

"And Mrs. Doll is braver still,
Wading a stream or climbing a hill.
The most beautiful Doll House Doll of all,
Wearing a leafy silver shawl
And a sun-helmet made of a flower white,
(You can take that off, my dear, at night).
Though she's torn on a twig,
And she's lacking a wig,
She's a beautiful beautiful beautiful beautiful beautiful
    beautiful sight!"

"What a pretty song, my dear!" said Mrs. Doll.

She, like Mr. Doll, was tired and frightened and discouraged. But the something in her heart that told her the children were alive and well, and the seven new leaf dresses she had worn since she left Coral Cottage, kept her from crying.

Each time she put on a new leaf she felt better.

She had one like green velvet lined with grey fur.

One, dark red with pale pink veins.

One (she liked this very much, and even stopped to admire its reflection in a pool) dark green, with beautiful points. On this was printed another leaf shape, just the same except that it was smaller, of dark purple; and on this a tiny leaf shape of pale purple.

One, yellow, with dark red edges. She called this, to herself, "My golden gown."

A grey one, that she called, "My silver gown."

A green one that sparkled in the sun as if it were powdered with diamond dust.

And one that was scarlet, covered with a network of pale yellow veins, like lace, and had a long point for a train. This was her favourite.

Does that make seven? Green. Red. Green. Yellow. Grey. Green. Scarlet.

One for every finger of your right hand, and one each for the thumb and finger of your left hand.

But Mr. Doll wouldn't change his leaves. He said real explorers didn't put on new suits seven times a day. Besides, he felt cooler after the twigs had torn away most of what he was wearing.

The only thing he would bother about was his sun-helmet.

He had just picked that up for the twenty-first time, when Mrs. Doll suddenly made a sound between a scream and a whisper, clutched his arm, and said, firmly:

"Be still!"

Chapter Thirty-One

THE MONKEY

Mr. Doll wanted to explain that he was being still, but before he could say so, Mrs. Doll went on:

"Look! Look!"

"Look where, my dear? Look at what?"

"There! A monkey! And I'm perfectly sure that's Dinah's dress he has on!"

A small grey-brown monkey sat huddled up on a branch, with his long tail dangling. He had a mournful pinky face, with a wrinkled forehead, surprised-looking dark eyebrows, and bright, sad tea-coloured eyes. His tiny ears were like very pale-pink wax.

He clung loosely to the branch above with one long-fingered pale-pink hand, and hunted for something in his fur with the other. The sleeves of Dinah's dress were tied around his neck, and the skirt spread over his back like a cape, pink, black, and yellow.

Then he found what he was hunting for, looked perfectly astonished, ate it, and swung himself to the next tree.

"We must follow him," Mrs. Doll whispered, forgetting all about following Mr. Doll's nose. "He may lead us to Dinah, and perhaps she will know where William and Annabel are."

Mr. and Mrs. Doll Follow the Monkey.

Mr. Doll.

So the Dolls crept after the monkey, their little feet treading lightly as the feet of birds.

He had not seen them, and so he was not in a hurry.

Mr. Doll went first, turning back every now and then to put his finger to his lips. This rather annoyed Mrs. Doll, who was keeping as quiet as he was, but she couldn't tell him so without making a noise and startling the monkey.

Oh, that monkey was tiring to follow! Either he was swinging from tree to tree so fast the Dolls had to run to keep up with him, or he was stopping for ever so long, to eat some fruit, to scratch, or to swing by his tail.

Mr. Doll picked two large leaves, and whenever the monkey paused to look around him, the Dolls would stand still, each holding a leaf, pretending to be a plant.

But the monkey caught sight of them. With a chatter, he swung down from a branch, snatched Mr. Doll's sun-helmet, leapt to the next tree, and vanished among the leaves.

Chapter Thirty-Two

THE SCARLET TRAIL

"Why did you let him go?" sobbed Mrs. Doll. "Now we'll *never* find Dinah and the children!"

Mr. Doll felt sad. He had lost two of his children, his sun-helmet, and the monkey, and now Mrs. Doll was crying.

He looked so discouraged that she put her arms around him and kissed him.

"Never mind!" she said. "We'll find them yet! We'll ask everyone we meet, even tigers! No one could help noticing a monkey in a plaid dress *and* a sun-helmet!"

There was a scream from the tree above them, but not a frightening one. It sounded kind, and as if it were asking a question.

They looked up to see a scarlet macaw, with her head on one side, gazing down at them out of friendly round bright eyes.

"Ask that red parrot if she has seen the monkey," whispered Mrs. Doll.

"She isn't a parrot, my dear, she's a macaw. Don't you remember in the Alphabet Book in the Toy Shop?

"M stands for Macaw, with her feathers so bright.
She has a sharp beak, so you'd best be polite!

"No, that wasn't quite the way it went. But, anyway, I know she's a macaw."

"Well, ask Mrs. Macaw."

Mr. Doll forgot, and tried to take off his sun-helmet. But he couldn't, because the monkey had it. So he bowed and said:

"Good morning, madam!"

"Afternoon, my dear," said Mrs. Doll.

"Good afternoon, madam. Sluvly afternoon."

"It—is—lovely," said Mrs. Doll, inside her head, not aloud, for Mr. Doll was still looking discouraged and she didn't want to make him feel worse.

The macaw screamed politely.

"Mrs. Doll and I ——"

Mrs. Doll here bowed, and said distinctly:

"How do you do, Mrs. Macaw? It is a love-ly afternoon, isn't it?"

The macaw screamed politely.

"Mrs. Doll and I are trying to find our son William and our daughter Annabel and our cook Dinah ——"

"We think they are lost in the jungle," Mrs. Doll broke in. "And we saw a monkey wearing Dinah's dress, so we followed him and then he —— *You* explain to the lady, my dear!"

"He stole my sun-helmet," Mr. Doll said. "And then ——"

"He simply vanished from sight!" Mrs. Doll began again. "And we haven't the least idea how to find him, and we don't even know where we are, ourselves. *Did* you notice which way he went? We would be *so* much obliged if you could direct us! Or *have* you any idea where our children are? Tell Mrs. Macaw what the children look like, my dear!"

"William is a boy, and Annabel is a girl, and Dinah is a cook. The monkey was rather small, and had on a plaid dress ——"

Mrs. Doll had kept her mouth open in order to begin talking the instant Mr. Doll stopped. But here she felt she must speak at once, or burst.

"*Dinah!* The *monkey!*" she said. "Upon my word! It was our *child*ren this lady was anxious to hear about, my dear! They are very remarkable children, Mrs. Macaw. I don't say that just because I'm their mother, for everyone speaks of it. My son William is a splendid boy doll, with brown china hair and very pink cheeks, and jointed all over. My dear little daughter Annabel is jointed, too, and both the children can turn their heads all the way round. You may think it is a mother's fondness, but indeed it is true that my daughter Annabel is a wonderfully beautiful child. Everyone says she looks exactly like me. She has pink cheeks and brown eyes and real hair, and all her underclothes are edged with the best and stiffest lace. And both of my children are so bright and so good! Not in the least like most children. So *if* you could help us find them, or at least show us which way the monkey went, because we are so anxious about them, and we really *ought* to be getting home, lovely as your jungle is, because we left our Baby—I *wish* you could see Baby, Mrs. Macaw, I know you would love him—with only two Crabs to look after him, delightful Crabs, and great friends of the family, but you know how helpless gentlemen are with a baby, and not a soul in our house but a caretaker, or I wouldn't be feeling so worried ——"

The macaw screamed politely and flew away.

"Well!" said Mrs. Doll. "She might have let me say just one *word* ——"

"I think she is showing us the way, my dear."

"But she's out of sight!"

"Yes, but she has dropped a feather. That is called a clew."

A scarlet feather lay on the ground. They hurried to it.

"We must follow the way it is pointing," said Mr. Doll.

Mrs. Doll started in that direction, but gave a jump as an Indian war-cry sounded behind her.

"Wah-wah-wah-wah-wah-wah-wah!"*

Turning, she saw it was Mr. Doll, who had tied the feather to his head with a vine tendril, and was pretending to be an Indian brave. Now he jumped up and down, whooping. Now he fell flat and pressed his ear to the ground, listening for enemies' footsteps.

"I'm Big Chief Hunt-a-Monkey," he explained. "You can be my Squaw Look-For-The-Cook."

But Mrs. Doll didn't feel like playing, so Mr. Doll had to be Indians all by himself.

"Oh, here's another of Mrs. Macaw's feathers!" cried Mrs. Doll.

"Wah-wah-wah-wah-wah-wah-wah!" whooped Mr. Doll. "I only speak Indian!"

* *This is almost it, but not quite. To hear how it really sounded, you must shout, and, while you are shouting, pat your hand over and over again in front of your mouth.*

"Never mind," said Mrs. Doll. "It isn't a feather, after all, it's only a little toadstool."

Mr. Doll.

Mr. Doll as an Indian.

"But anything scarlet is a clew," Mr. Doll said. "That is a rule."

"I never heard it before," Mrs. Doll objected.

"Probably not. I just made it up this minute," said Mr.

Doll, firmly. "It is a very good rule, because it is so fresh. You know that fresh rolls are the best rolls, don't you?"

"Yes, my dear."

"Well, fresh rules are the best rules. The motto of this search is, Follow the Scarlet Clew!"

And Mr. Doll walked on, singing:

"Up the woods and over the woods and under the woods and
     through,
 Though monkeys may gambol we'll quietly ramble in search of
     a scarlet clew!"

Sometimes, when he went on ahead, Mrs. Doll would catch a gleam of scarlet, and run to it, thinking she had found another clew.

And it was always Mr. Doll and his feather. So disappointing!

Often they found small scarlet orchids, trailing up grey tree-trunks. But they decided not to count them as clews, for they would have led up into the sky or off the tips of branches.

"No more clews. We must follow my nose again," said Mr. Doll, with a sigh, for he was growing terribly tired.

Mrs. Doll sighed also. She was almost too tired to speak, but not quite.

"My dear, do you think our caretaker will let strangers

go through the Doll House? Of course there will be a lot of curiosity about such a grand new place on the beach."

"It would be too hard to get into it."

"Not for a flying-fish, or a sea gull. My *dear!* There was a very suspicious-looking sea gull on the beach last night. He kept looking into the kitchen while I was getting supper. I spoke to him, perfectly pleasantly at first, and said we had nothing to give him, and we didn't want to buy anything, seaweed, or shrimps, or *any*thing, but he wouldn't go away. So I chased him, but he would just fly a little way, and come back the minute I went into the kitchen again. *Do* you suppose he was the sea gull who stole Dinah, and that he will come back to steal Baby?"

"I don't believe so. The Crabs will take care of Baby."

"Do you suppose they'll know enough to give him his evening bottle?"

Mr. Doll hoped they would.

"What *do* crabs give their babies for supper?"

"Dead fish, I suppose. But don't worry."

"Don't worry!" thought Mrs. Doll. And she began to cry quietly, in spite of being afraid that tears might melt her wax eyelids, for if she felt so lost and lonely, with Mr. Doll to take care of her, what must Annabel be feeling? And William? Her little lost children! And Baby, who had

They Slept in Two Flower-cups, and Mr. Doll Thought It Was Fun, and Mrs.
Doll Didn't

never been given anything but bottles of the freshest air, perhaps having jellyfish for supper!

Something was happening in the jungle. Far off in the tree-tops they heard a sound like the washing in of a gentle wave. The leaves, that had hung heavy and silent all day, began to stir and speak to one another.

All along the path of the Dolls rose tall white toadstools with cone-shaped tops and silky stems. They were so tall that the Dolls could look up into their deeply pleated linings. Others were silently pushing through, some showing white, some still hidden, but lifting the earth in mounds, and making it heave beneath the Dolls' feet.

The light of the day was growing dim, but the Dolls could still see the colours around them—linings of toadstools so pale a pink, big fluttering moths so pale a green, that they were almost white.

Dew sparkled softly on cobwebs, turning them into crystal wheels.

Mrs. Doll leaned against a toadstool, feeling peaceful again.

Sometime they would all be together. Until then, she would look for her children, if it took years and years.

She and Mr. Doll slept in two flower cups that night, and Mr. Doll thought it was fun, and Mrs. Doll didn't.

All the next day they pushed through the jungle, and they found two scarlet clews. Another of Mrs. Macaw's feathers, and a bush full of berries, clear as glass, with seeds showing dark inside of them.

They slept in a cobweb hammock that night, and got all tangled up in it. Mr. Doll thought it was fun, and Mrs. Doll didn't.

The next day they hunted again, all day long, and found two more clews. A vine with scarlet trumpet flowers, that looped from tree to tree, and a scarlet beetle, very friendly, that led them for ever so long.

When it was too dark to see the beetle any more, Mrs. Doll heard Mr. Doll crying, excitedly:

"My dear! Come quickly! Hurry! Run as fast as you can! Just *see* what I've found!"

Chapter Thirty-Three

THE FRIGHTENING FLOWERS

Now, if you please, we will go back to William in the Land Crab's hole, with the Land Crab sitting on top of the opening.

William was frightened.

But he wasn't going to let the Land Crab know it.

First he sang "The Bluebells of Scotland," which he, like Mr. Doll, had learned from the Music Box in the Toy Shop.

The Land Crab kicked a little dirt down on him.

That was discouraging, but it didn't stop William, who now began to recite.

He recited:

> "Politeness is to do or say
> The kindest thing in the kindest way!"

and the two table up to two times five, and the alphabet.

The Land Crab kicked down some more dirt.

William shook it off his head, and began to talk to himself, very loud, so the Land Crab should hear:

"My father is the bravest doll in the world. Everybody in the world is afraid of my father. He is coming to get me, and he isn't afraid of anything! All the crabs in the world do just what my father tells them. If he wanted a ride, do you know what he would do? He would ride crab-back. He would stand up with one foot on one crab, and the other on another crab, and make them go like lightning wherever he told them, and he would never fall off. My father could make lions and tigers and crocodiles and boa-constrictors and whales and dormice and crabs do tricks and sit up and beg and hold lumps of sugar on their noses and roll over. My father ——"

The Land Crab shovelled a great deal of dirt on top of William.

William meant to stay awake all night, and never stop talking a minute, just to show he wasn't frightened. He wanted to frighten the Land Crab, instead.

But he fell asleep, and dreamed that the Snail came down the hole, wearing Mrs. Doll's wig and her ball-gown, with the train trailing along behind.

"Mother won't like that!" said William, so the Snail took off the wig, and there was Pudding, sitting in it like a bird in its nest, singing "The Bluebells of Scotland." And when he had finished his song, an Ant presented him with a bouquet of a white flower fringed with ferns, and all the good Crabs sang "The Blue Claws of Crabland." The Green Lizard sang, too, his throat swelling out in a yellow bubble—bigger and bigger, until—*Bang!*—it burst, and William woke up, and found the sun pouring on him.

The Land Crab must have gone away!

William pulled himself out.

And there was the Land Crab, beside his hole, with a cruel claw darting out!

William ran—oh, how he ran! And the Land Crab came after him, so close that once the tip of his claw scraped down William's back.

Here was a sloping dead tree-trunk, with tufts of fern to pull by.

Up went William.

Up came the Crab.

The tree leaned over the water, and a vine looped and twisted around it, full of huge thick heart-shaped leaves and frightening flowers.*

* *These flowers have a long name and a short name. You know what I mean. Just as a little boy might be named Richard Alexander Throckmorton, and be called Dicky, or a*

The flowers frightened William almost as much as the Land Crab did. How shall I make you see them as he saw them?

The baby Duppy cups didn't frighten him. They were as small as your finger nail, and green as the leaves they hid against, and they looked like some of the strange little sea-creatures he had watched in the old Crab's pool.

The middle ones, shaded from pale green to white, didn't frighten him badly.

little girl might be named Louisa Mary Tillingford, and be called Sister.

Their long name is the Aristolochia flower.

Their short name—at least, so Elizabeth says—is Duppy cup.

Do you remember Elizabeth? She is the little girl who lives on a cocoa plantation, and her Uncle Henry bought the Doll House and the Family for her birthday present.

Elizabeth says the brown people think Duppies are bad fairies, who live in the jungle where the Duppy cups grow. Elizabeth doesn't know whether she believes in Duppies. She knows there are Duppy cups, because she has seen them. But she has looked for Duppies all her life (nearly nine years) and she has never caught a glimpse of one.

But the big ones, big as your father's two hands spread side by side, made him shiver.

He looked at the one nearest him. From a purple stem hung a swelling tube, palest green, ridged with pale purple-brown veins. The tube grew narrow, twisted, and, swelling again, lifted, like an animal lifting its head, to spread into a huge ridged white shell, each purple-brown ridge joined with a network of purple-brown veins, and twisting into a long narrow tendril that dangled far, far down. And it had an open purple throat, deep and dark as a tunnel, that looked as if it would pull him in and never let him out again.

He didn't know what to do.

"If the Land Crab catches me, he'll put me down in his hole, and never let me out! If I get into that flower to hide, I think it will eat me!* If I fall into the water ———"

*Perhaps you think William was silly to think a flower could eat anything, but Duppy cups do eat flies and little insects. This is the way they catch them: The flowers are like pitchers full of a liquid that smells delicious to flies, so in they come for a meal, and then they can't get out, for it is as sticky as fly-paper. Then, instead of their making a meal in the Duppy cup, the Duppy cup makes a meal of them.

He looked down.

It was a long way, but he might jump, climb up on that old log, and get to the shore before the Land Crab could reach him.

The old log suddenly opened its jaws, showing rows of sharp white teeth, and clapped them together again, with a sound as loud as the firing of a cannon, before it slithered and scrambled half out on the bank.

It was a Crocodile!

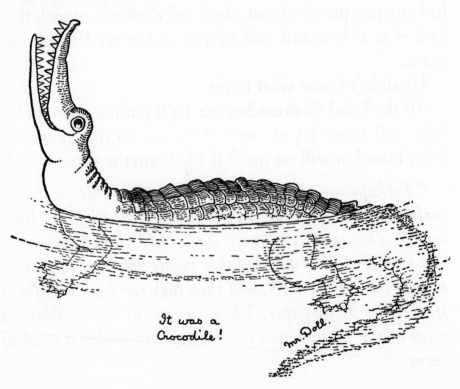

It was a
Crocodile!

mr Doll.

Chapter Thirty-Four

THE RAIN

A cloud like a dragon had swallowed the sun, and now it spread until the sky was first blue-black as ink, then mud-colour. There was a breathless silence.

Suddenly a Duppy cup beside William bowed, and although he was weak in the joints from the fright the Crocodile had given him, William remembered his manners, put his heels together and his hand over his heart, and bowed back, as his mother had taught him to bow to Annabel when he asked:

"May I have the pleasure of this waltz?"

But he didn't put out his tongue at the Duppy cup, as he sometimes did at Annabel, just to keep her from feeling too airy.

Another Duppy cup bowed. A leaf jumped. They were all bowing and leaping.

Then, *splash!* a big warm drop spatted on William's head. It was rain that was making the leaves and flowers bow.

Wind screamed like a wildcat, thunder roared louder than a jungleful of tigers, clapped louder than the jaws of a riverful of crocodiles.

mr. Doll.

William's Bird.

Rain fell in crystal rods, churning the water, turning it to smoke, hanging veils between William and the rest of the world. He was nearly washed from his branch. He could not have seen or heard the Land Crab if it had been only the thickness of a leaf away.

Then the hiss and roar of the rain changed to a chiming

William Bows to the Duppy-Cup

drip-drop, sunlight made wet leaves shine and gleamed on the bright purple, vermilion, and yellow of the Land Crab, the length of your hand from William.

A cruel claw darted out like lightning towards him.

William heard a sudden soft twitter.

A small grey bird with a flame-coloured breast and beak was beating the air in front of him with flame-lined grey wings.

William flung his arms around the bird's neck, and swung himself to its back, just as the Land Crab reached the spot where he had stood.

With a swoop that nearly knocked the astonished Land Crab off the branch, the bird soared up above the tree-tops, into the sky, where now a beautiful rainbow arched.

Chapter Thirty-Five

IN THE SKY

At first William lay exhausted, his head down on the bird's smooth neck, his arms deep in soft breast-feathers.

The feeling of safety, the air flowing by, the kind little heart beating under his hands, filled him with happiness and made him strong again. He gazed down. They were flying so high that the jungle looked like moss, with here and there a blossoming tree so far down and tiny that it seemed to be one little flower. Streams were twisted silver wires, pools were bits of looking-glass. So high that at last William saw the whole island like a bouquet edged with white foam, floating in the bright blue sea.

Now the island rose up to them, moss turned to trees again, trees turned to big wet leaves looking as if they had been cut with scissors into curious shapes, and to clusters of flowers in which he could see pools of rain-water shining. A monkey in a tree-top was so close that William could see the hairs of his small black fur cap, and the surprised look in his tea-coloured eyes. And now William was look-

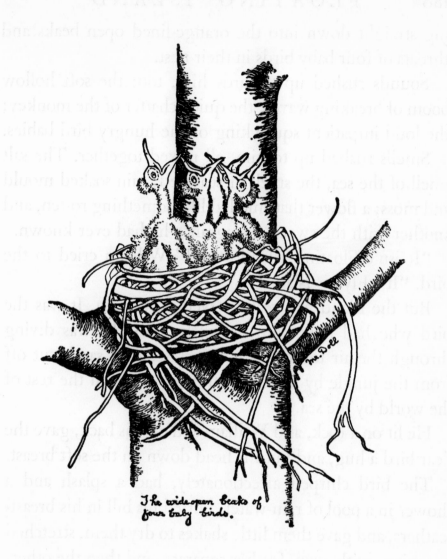

The wide open beaks of
four baby birds.

ing straight down into the orange-lined open beaks and throats of four baby birds in their nest.

Sounds rushed up towards him, too: the soft hollow boom of breaking waves; the quick chatter of the monkey; the loud impatient squawking of the hungry bird babies.

Smells rushed up to him, all mixed together. The salt smell of the sea, the smell of seaweed; rain-soaked mould and moss; a flower that smelled like something rotten, and another with the sweetest fragrance he had ever known.

"It isn't Floating Island at all!" William cried to the bird. "It's Flying Island!"

But the island had really stayed on the sea. It was the bird who had flown down swiftly. Now he was diving through the air towards a white crescent of sand, cut off from the jungle by tall cliffs, and cut off from the rest of the world by the sea.

He lit on a rock, and William slid off his back, gave the dear bird a hug, and put his head down on the soft breast.

The bird chirped affectionately, had a splash and a shower in a pool of rain-water, buried his bill in his breast-feathers, and gave them little shakes to dry them, stretched one wing, with every feather separate, and then the other, as you would stretch your arms after carrying something heavy. The light of the setting sun struck his breast and the insides of his wings until they seemed to be on fire.

Then, with a soft sudden whirr, he was off.

William stood on the rock, still feeling rather shaky, to look after his friend.

Up, up, happy and free, dipping and diving and soaring in a sky that seemed full of flame-coloured feathers from the dear bird's breast. Little feathery clouds burned in the sunset, that laid flame-coloured feathers between the blue-green ridges of the sea, and turned the foam of the breaking waves to gold.

"Good-bye, my Bird!" William called.

But the bird was gone.

Chapter Thirty-Six

THE COOK'S SHOE

Now we are going to learn what happened to Annabel.

When the box that held the Doll House was broken on the rocks, Annabel was pulled back into the sea, rolled here, rolled there, and at last washed up on a beach with some shells and an old shoe that had belonged to the cook of *The Pride of the Waves,* and that he hadn't had time to put on before he got into a life-boat.

She was terribly frightened and lonely, but she was a brave little doll, and tried to make the best of things until William came, for she was sure, all the time, that he would find her somehow.

She could discover no way of leaving her beach.

First came the sea.

Then the sand, with a few cocoanut-palms leaning out as if they, like Annabel, wanted to escape and were looking for a ship.

Then more sand.

Then cactus plants, dreadfully prickly, and a few sea-grapes with thick grey-green and purple leaves.

The Cactus needles tore Annabel's Clothes.

Then, like a curving wall to keep her a prisoner, the high cliff, too smooth and bare to climb.

All day and all night hot wind blew in from the sea, tearing the palm-leaves into strings, covering cactus and sea-grape leaves with fine white sand, and rattling sharp tiny grains of sand against Annabel. Her hair was full of them, they were ground into her wax eyelids, and even got into her joints and made them stiff. The only way of getting out of the wind was to crawl into the cook's old shoe, which lay on its side on the beach.

The long sharp cactus needles had torn her clothes so badly, when she first ran among them, trying to escape from the beach, that they were no good for anything but signal flags. Some of them fluttered from the cactus spines, and one streamer (with a lace edge) she fastened to the cook's shoe, hoping that a ship might see it and come in to rescue her.

There wasn't much for Annabel to do each day, after she had made her seaweed bed in the cook's shoe.

Sometimes she practised writing her name in the dust on the sea-grape leaves, but by the time she finished the "Doll," new dust had covered the "Annabel."

She made herself a seaweed dress.

She printed the names of all the family on the sand with sea-shells, to keep her company.

"FATHER" was made of pale green shells, like moth-wings.

"MOTHER" of pale pink ones, like wild-rose petals.

"WILLIAM" of curly freckled ones.

Annabel in the Cook's Shoe

"BABY" of round red ones, like tiny raspberries.

"DINAH" of chocolate-coloured ones.

There was only one pleasant place on the windy hot beach, so hot that Annabel was afraid her wax eyelids would melt. This was a rock pool, where tiny fish, transparent as glass, swam in and out dark clots of seaweed, and mussel and scallop shells, fastened to the side of the rock, seemed to smile at the little doll. Here lived a shrimp, a pale pink little creature with long waving feelers. Annabel named the shrimp Rosy, and loved her dearly.

But it was a sad and lonely little doll who sat in the doorway of her shoe house, listening to the waves and to the blown sand rattling against torn palm-leaves, and looking at the enormous John crows who sailed like black clouds in the sky, or perched in the trees at the top of the cliff, stretching out ugly bare necks, and spreading first one long wing and then the other in the sunshine. And each night Annabel saw the stars through tears that made them blur and tremble.

Chapter Thirty-Seven

SUPPER BY MOONLIGHT

When his bird flew out of sight, William turned from the sea and looked at the beach.

There lay an old shoe. As he watched, something pink stuck out from it.

"Another crab," William thought, and jumped down from the rock to have a look.

But you know it wasn't a crab. It was Annabel.

They hugged each other. They jumped up and down. And still they couldn't believe it.

William kept saying:

"Annabel!"

And Annabel kept saying:

"William!"

Then William said:

"I flew here on a bird! We went miles high in the sky, and when we came down we nearly hit a monkey!"

And Annabel said:

"I have the darlingest pet shrimp! She has l-o-n-g whiskers, and she's pink, and her name is Rosy!"

They were both talking together, at the tops of their voices, so if you had been there you would have heard something like this:

"I flew here on a—pet shrimp—we went miles high in the—whiskers—and when we came down we nearly hit a —pink—monkey—and her name is Rosy!"

If Mrs. Doll had been there, she would certainly have put her hands over her ears, and said:

"Gently, children, gently! No one is deaf!"

So they decided they had better take turns in telling each other all that had happened. Annabel said "Ladies first!" so many times that William thought he might as well let her begin; and every time she stopped for breath he told part of his story.

Annabel said: "The name of this beach is Annabel's Beach."

William said: "How do you know?"

"I *do* know!"

"Well, I came part way along a river, and the name of it is William's River."

"How do you know?"

"I *do* know!"

So that was settled.

"And there isn't any way of leaving Annabel's Beach."

"I *flew* down," said William.

"Let's see you fly up!"

"Oh, well," said William.

"But now that you've come, I'm not frightened any more. We can camp out together. There's lots of room in my shoe."

"No one can say, 'Bedtime, children!' "

"Oh, *William,* I'm glad you found me!"

While they were talking, the big white moon rose, turning sea and sand to silver, and giving so bright a light that Annabel could show William everything—her shoe house, her signal flags, and Rosy in the rock pool.

When Annabel said:

"Here's my brother William, Rosy! You know I told you he would come!" Rosy looked as if she were bowing. So William put his heels together, and his hand over his heart, and bowed too, as he had bowed to the Duppy cup.

Then they sat down to supper, and had everything they liked but weren't often allowed.

For, you see, all they had to do was to choose what the air should be, in their shell cups and dishes. When they had supper in the Doll House, Mrs. Doll always decided what the air was, and it was never anything more exciting than milk-toast or apple-sauce.

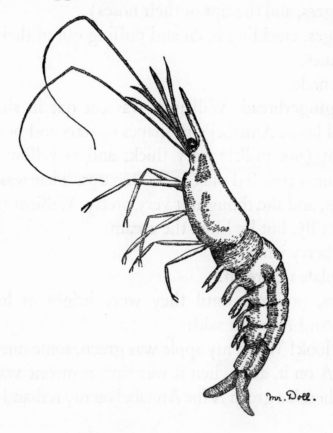

mr. Doll.

Rosy makes a Bow.

But this time William and Annabel decided the air should be:

Buttered toast (very hot, with a great deal of butter, so much that it oozed out through the under side, and got on their fingers, and the tips of their noses).

Sausages, crackling open and puffing out of their skins.

Pancakes.

Lemonade.

Hot gingerbread. William's was cut out in shapes of men and lions, Annabel's in shapes of stars and hearts.

Cream (not milk!) very thick, and as yellow as if it came from a cow fed only on buttercups. That was Annabel's idea, and she thought it very pretty. William thought it rather silly, but he liked the cream.

Blackberry jam.

Chocolate ice cream.

Apples, polished until they were bright as looking-glasses. And Annabel said:

"Oh, look! While my apple was green, some one pasted a paper A on it, and when it was ripe, someone washed it off, and here's a green A for Annabel on my red-and-yellow apple!"

"And here's a W for William on mine!"

Then they had chocolate cigarettes.

Annabel had cocoa, but William was naughty and had coffee, cups of it! Annabel wished she had thought of that first, because it seemed so grand and grown-up, but since she hadn't she pretended she would *rather* have cocoa.

They sat up long past their bedtime.

Annabel thought they ought to start back that night. But William thought it would be fun to live on the beach for a year or so, before they tried to find the others. He liked having ice-cream air and lemonade air for supper, and sitting up late, and not wearing even a leaf, and he wanted to teach Rosy and the little fish tricks, and perhaps see his bird again.

"Mother and Father will be worried about us, William."

"No, they won't, Annabel, because when I ran away I wrote on the sand, 'Don't worry.'"

At last they decided to wait until morning, and then try to find some way of leaving Annabel's Beach.

So they lay down in the cook's shoe, and Annabel said:

"Good night, William! Sweet dreams!"

"Good night, Annabel! But I'm not going to sleep all night long. I don't have to do anything I don't want to. Maybe I'll go swimming by moonlight. Maybe I'll go and play with those little fish."

"I'm going to sleep. Good night, William. William, good night! Are you asleep?"

William was fast asleep.

Chapter Thirty-Eight

FINNY'S BEACH

William was still so fast asleep next morning that Annabel shouted, *"Boo!"* without being able to wake him.

So she ran down to the sea, scooped up as much of it as would go in a scallop-shell, and poured it over him.

That made him sit up!

"Oh, you Sleepy-head!"

"I wasn't asleep! I was thinking."

"What were you thinking about?"

"I was thinking how to get away from your beach, and now I've thought. We must swim around the point of the cliffs."

"Oh, William, I can't!"

"Yes, you can. We'll make life-preservers out of seaweed air-bubbles, and then all we have to do is keep on kicking."

"Shall we take Rosy? She can swim."

"But a shrimp couldn't walk through the jungle, Annabel."

"She'll miss me so!"

"Oh, she probably has a family," said William. "We'll find another shrimp for you on Doll House Beach."

"Another shrimp won't be Rosy," said Annabel, sadly.

They went to Rosy's Pool to say good-bye to her. The little shrimp bowed and waved her feelers, and Annabel nearly cried.

"I'll come back and see you some day," she said. "Darling, *darling* Rosy!"

Then William and Annabel left the beach, with the shoe house, and "MOTHER," "FATHER," "WILLIAM," "BABY," and "DINAH" written in coloured shells on the sand, and unless the waves have washed them away, I suppose they are still there, on the little island somewhere in the big blue sea.

After all, Annabel enjoyed the swim. She and William had splendid luck, for William managed to catch hold of the filmy tail of a little Fish, who looked as if his mother had dressed him in a bright new suit of turquoise-blue and silver scales that morning. Annabel caught William's foot, and—*whish!*—they swept through the clear water, with no trouble at all.

I think little Fish must have thought some strange kind of crab had caught hold of his tail. He did everything to make William let go. He swam down, and up, and in a

wavy line, and leaped into the air. Behind him swished
William and Annabel, down, up, in a wavy line, and into
the air, while bubbles fizzed and streamed behind them.

The Little Fish.
Father made this picture,
but we helped him.
William.
ANNABEL.

You and I couldn't have done it, for we need air to
breathe, but dolls can breathe under water just as well as
above it.

Little Fish gave such a high leap that William had time to see another beach, from which the jungle sloped easily up and away. As Fish dove under again, William dropped his tail and tried to say, "Thank you!" But the words turned into two bubbles: "Blub blub."

Their air-bladder life-preservers shot them up to the top of the sea.

William looked towards Annabel, and saw only two black china slippers, two white china socks, two pink china knees, pointed to the sky. She had risen feet first, and it took a lot of diving and pushing and pulling before William got her right way up.

The waves lazily rolled them up on the beach, and then pulled back the sand from under them. They sat in a froth of bursting bubbles.

"Oh, wouldn't Dinah like all these soapsuds to do the washing with!" said Annabel.

"Now, into the jungle!" cried William.

"Wait a minute," said Annabel, taking off the bit of seaweed she had tied around her head to keep her wig dry.

"Oh, hurry *yup!*" called William, beginning to push into the green twilight.

"Wait a minute," said Annabel, washing the sand from her china shoes.

"Hurry *yup!*" William shouted, going on.

"Wait a minute! William! William! Come back! I've found something! William!"

"I can't hear you!"

"Come *back!* I've found—I think I've found —— *Will*iam!"

William came back, grumbling.

Annabel was digging in the sand, so fast that it flew in a shower.

"I saw an eye! Just one eye, looking up at me, and I think —*help* me dig! I think it is—yes, it *is* Finny!"

Chapter Thirty-Nine

A VOICE IN THE DARK

Finny had lost his cardboard plate, and was so covered with sand that he looked as if he had been rolled in bread-crumbs, ready for frying. But otherwise he was all right. He was even wearing his three slices of plaster lemon. They were so glad to see him!

Now, which was the way home?

William didn't know. If he could find his River, that would lead him. But how should he find it?

He heard Annabel saying:

"Finny, William is perfectly wonderful! He came straight through the jungle and found me, and he isn't afraid of anything, even big bad crabs and crocodiles. What did you say?" For she insisted she could understand Finny, and Lobby, Chicky, and Pudding, too. She was always answering their questions. But William thought that was easy, because she asked their questions for them.

"Where is your Dinah? Dinah's flown away with a sea gull, but William is going to find her and bring her back.

197

And now he's going to take us straight home to Mother and
Father and Baby and Pudding and Chicky and Lobby."

William couldn't take time to be frightened, with Annabel and Finny depending on him.

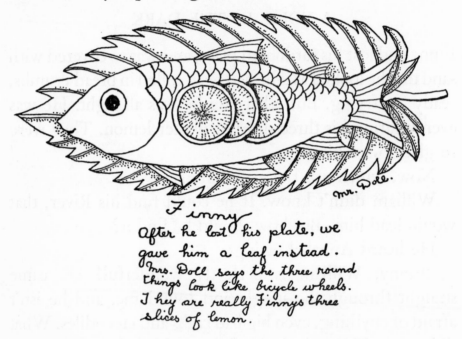

Finny
After he lost his plate, we
gave him a leaf instead.
Mrs. Doll says the three round
things look like bicycle wheels.
I hey are really Finny's three
slices of lemon.

He started out as if he knew where he was going, and
Annabel trotted behind him, taking first turn at carrying
Finny, and telling him all about the other fish, the blue and
silver one who had given them such an exciting swim.

This part of the island wasn't any more pleasant than
Annabel's Beach.

First came jagged rocks of scratching coral.

Then a bare waste of red dust, hot in the sun, that rose in clouds as they ploughed through it, and stuck to their bodies, still wet from the sea.

Then a forest of dusty cactus plants, taller than grown-up men.

And all the time they had to fight their way through clouds of shrilly-buzzing insects.

You and I would have been badly bitten. Sometimes it must be a comfort to be made of china.

Then, at last, cool ferns, grey with dew.

Finny had been getting heavier

and *heavier*

and HEAVIER,

and Annabel paused to rest in the shade, lost sight of William, ran to catch up, and took a wrong turn.

Oh, she was glad she had! She called:

"Come and see what I've found! Kittens!"*

Three furry balls were curled up in a nest of flattened ferns. Annabel and William stood on tiptoe and patted as much as they could reach, and the cubs patted back with

* *These were tiger cubs, the babies of the tiger Mr. and Mrs. Doll mistook for a grove of trees.*

soft balls of paws. One stretched and yawned until its eyes closed to liquid slits, and its pink tongue curled. One rolled on its back with its paws in the air. One gave a jump, to show how well it could catch a shadow.

Annabel wanted to take them all to the Doll House.

What was that roar?*

"Thunder!" William cried. "Run, Annabel! Here's a cave we can wait in until the storm is over."

Annabel hated leaving her kittens, especially one, that flopped along, trying to follow them. But she didn't want to be lost again, so she ran after William.

The opening he had found was as low as if you had taken a croquet mallet and knocked a wicket nearly into the ground. They had to lie flat to wiggle through, but inside the cave was high and deep. Dark, too. Annabel couldn't see William at all.

"Where are you?" she called, and heard a faint voice, far away, call back:

* *You know what it was, don't you? It was the tiger cubs' mother coming home to them through the jungle, and roaring as she came. It would sound frightening and fierce to you and me, but the tiger's babies thought it the pleasantest sound in the world.*

"Where are you?"

At the same moment William bumped into her. He was so near, and the voice she had thought his was so distant, that she screamed.

Far off they heard another scream.

"Some one is lost in the cave!" Annabel whispered.

"We must find him!" William whispered back.

They went farther in, then stood still to listen.

Everywhere around them they heard faint rustlings, whisperings, the drip of water.

"Hello!" shouted William.

"Hello!" shouted the voice, as far away as before.

"Stand still, and we'll find you!"

"We'll find you!"

So William and Annabel stood still, and again there was nothing but whispering, rustling darkness.

"Let's go farther," said William; so hand in hand the two little dolls went through the dark, feeling their way along slippery wet rocks. Drops of water began to fall— *spat!*—on their heads.

"Where are you?" William shouted again.

But this time there was no answer.

"They've found their way out! They didn't wait for

us!" Annabel sobbed. "Oh, William, I'm frightened! Let's go back!"*

So they tried to find their way back.

They felt along the walls, and slipped ——

And slid ——

And stumbled ——

And when they stood still there was only darkness, full of rustling and whispering and dripping.

They were as lost as lost could be.

You have guessed what it was, haven't you?
If you haven't, take the first letter of each of these words:

Exciting
Curious
Hidden
Odd

And the word the letters spell is the name of what was answering William and Annabel.

Chapter Forty

THE WITCH'S CAVE

You see, tunnels led from the cave to other caves, and the dolls had gone on in the darkness under the earth, getting deeper in with every step.

"I mustn't let Annabel know how frightened I am!" thought William.

"I mustn't let William know how frightened I am!" thought Annabel. And, because she had said she was frightened, she now said, very cheerfully, but with a loud hiccuping sob in the middle:

"This is fun!"

Hand in hand went the two little dolls, close to the slippery wall. Once William's foot shot off into space. Pulling it back, he felt around carefully. They were on a narrow ledge of rock, and far below, as they stood still, they heard flowing water.

They crept on. The rushing of water grew louder.

Then they saw a faint light. Clinging to the ledge, they

came out from terrifying, whispering darkness into a big dim cave with a river running out of it.

They saw strange pale beasts watching them motionlessly; and a white witch with hunched-up knees and enormous head, her face flickering as if she were frowning, smiling, whispering to herself.*

The high arched roof was netted with reflected, quivering light, and bats hung from it, looking like rotten pears, or spread the small umbrellas of their wings and swooped, with squeaking cries, nearly knocking the dolls from their ledge into the water.

A downy white owl flew past them, crying: "Who-o-o?"

And William answered, in a voice he tried to make brave:

The beasts and the witch were not alive, as William and Annabel thought, but were the stone shapes of stalactites and stalagmites, coloured white and grey and pinkish yellow. The witch's face seemed to move because the reflection of water moved on it. Stalactites sometimes hang down from the tops of caves, and stalagmites rise up under them from the bottom, slowly built by drippings from the stalactites. There are two good big words for you!

"William and Annabel Doll!"
Out through the mouth of the cave they followed the

a white Owl asked
"Who-o-o?"

I told Father what
it looked like.
William.

SO DID I! ANNABEL.

river, that escaped in bright waterfalls over rocks green
with moss. Oh, the joy of coming into a blaze of sunlight

that blinded them at first! The rush of crystal water, bubbling and foaming, the whistling of birds, the flowering trees moving and lifting and shaking out their fragrance on the sweet hot air!

William looked at Annabel, and Annabel looked at William, and they both looked at Finny.

All three were covered with grey cobwebs and green slime; but who cared? They were so happy!

"I know this is my River!" said William. "It will lead us home!"

Chapter Forty-One

WILLIAM'S RIVER

Although they felt they had spent hours in the cave, it was still morning. Mist was caught among the trees, and lay on the surface of the River like a layer of cotton-wool; and the dewy flowers spilled water as if they were crying.

But the sun made a rainbow on the waterfall spray where they took a shower-bath.

Annabel tried to catch the rainbow. It was so lovely, she wanted to take it home as a present for her mother. She thought she had it. But she looked again, and only had spray on her hands.

"Never mind," said William. "We have a rainbow of our own, in the waterfall near Coral Cottage. Now we must make a raft."

So they gathered twigs, and bound them together with rootlets. Then they climbed aboard. William poled the raft away from the shore with another twig, and William's River drew them smoothly and swiftly along.

Tall wading-birds, with funny shapes, long bills, and lovely feathers like white and rose sunrise clouds, stood in

A Wading-Bird looks at William
and Annabel.

the shallows, and looked up from their fishing to see William and Annabel pass.

First the raft went between bamboo trees, that creaked and rattled and groaned, and made sounds as if corks were being pulled out of bottles. Then, mixed through the bamboos and palms and tree-ferns came enormous trees whose branches, covered with orchids, and tied by lianas, were woven together until they hid the sky, and made a tunnel through which the River flowed, looking as solid as a black glass floor, except where dipping branches frilled the water.

Over and over they thought, "This is the end of the River!" For the trees would seem to make a solid wall ahead. But the current swung them silently round a curve, and there was another stretch of dark water, and new things to see, as if a page of a book full of bright strange pictures had been turned.

A tree full of shaken-out flowers like tassels of carved ivory, and packed-up flowers still in their white kid bud-cases, where whole families of caterpillars with crimson feathery horns on their heads and tails were stuffing themselves.

A tree full of big black birds with bright yellow beaks, and bright yellow tail-feathers. One wove the bottom of his nest, that was like a long hanging basket; one sat looking out of the top of hers, as if she were a present in the top of a Christmas stocking; one fed her bird baby, who squawked and screeched and flapped with eagerness. There must have been a hundred hanging baskets of nests in that tree.*

A bird-of-paradise, with a tail like a drifting cloud of yellow smoke, floated over a tall plant whose thick smooth green stems curved down to hold crowns of bright yellow flowers, from which fell big pear-shaped sticky drops.**

And, dipping long slender beaks into every flower, bathing in every small waterfall, or quivering in the air as if they were hung on fine wires, everywhere were the humming-birds. So beautiful, so tiny, so swift, so brilliant, that William and Annabel hardly believed they were real. Such purple breasts, and blue, and green, and gold, flashing, changing colour, as they hung in air, held up by wings beating so fast that they turned to blurs!

They found a humming-bird's lichen-covered nest, lined with silky seed-down, hanging over the water, fastened to

These birds are the Crested Cassiques.

**This is the Aloe, or Century Plant. It only blooms every hundred years. William and Annabel were lucky! Suppose it had bloomed the year before. They would have had to wait ninety-nine years to see it.*

a spray of maidenhair fern by a rope of twisted cobweb. It was the size of a thimble. Annabel wanted to take it to her mother, for a hat.

"Annabel, you know Mother wouldn't wear a bird's nest!"

"Well, Father would!"

"I don't think Mother would like him to. Anyway, Father has a sun-helmet now."

"Then I'll take it for a work-basket for Dinah."

But she decided to leave it, when William said the humming bird might come back to look for it.

Each time William and Annabel (and Finny, too, Annabel said) wanted to look and look, the River swung their raft around a curve and showed them something else.

A liana (they thought) hanging from a tree, began to move. It slipped into the water, and they saw it was a swimming snake.

Things on that island were always turning out to be something else.

The snake swam straight towards the raft.

"Hold tight!" William shouted, catching up Finny.

Over went the raft, tipping them into the River.

Chapter Forty-Two

THE CAVE IN THE ROOTS

That part of the River was full of blue water-lilies, with leaves like green tea-trays, so big and strong that if you are quite small you could have stood on one.

Annabel, and William with Finny still under his arm, climbed on a leaf, and the families of insects that lived in the water-lilies ran and flew to see the dolls, and buzzed to one another about them.

The snake had disappeared, but far down the River swept the empty raft.

"We'll have to make another," William said. So they walked to shore across the green islands of lily-leaves, climbing the walls of their lifted rims, and politely bowing right and left to the crowds of interested insects.

Just as they reached the shore—*swish!*—down fell something small and bright, that looked like silver.

It was the cream-jug from the Doll House tea-set!

They looked up. For a second, bright eyes looked back, through parted branches.

Annabel, William, and Finny among the Water-lilies

"Is it Father?" Annabel gasped. For who else had a right to be carrying the cream-jug, except Mother. And Mother wouldn't be running around in the tree-tops.

"I saw something curled up at the end, that looked like a tail!"

"Maybe Father was carrying a cane!"

"No, it's a monkey!" William shouted. "See! There he is again! Run, Annabel! You take the cream-jug, and I'll bring Finny!"

They ran, their eyes turned up towards the dancing branches.

"I—don't—care! I—*still*—think—it's *Fath*er!" Annabel cried, her words joggling out of her.

Whoof! William tripped, and fell, and Annabel fell on top of him.

They picked themselves up. The leaves above them were still. They had lost Father or the monkey, whichever it was.

The tree that tripped them had lifted itself until it seemed to be standing tiptoe on roots covered with lichens; blue-grey cups, tiny dots of lemon-yellow, and flat fans of pale rose. Small clusters of ferns, too, had planted themselves all up its trunk. Among the lifted roots were little caves, and in front of the biggest, under a fern that sprang up in curves like a fountain, stood ——

One of the best red chairs from the Doll House!
It was covered with beads of dew, and looked like a rasp-

mr. Doll.

William and Annabel
find the Cave in the Roots.

berry after rain. Beside it grew a small toadstool, just right
for a table.

William and Annabel stared at each other, too surprised to speak.

Then they tiptoed under a big violet lichen, that curved out like the roof of a porch and into one of the caves.

There stood the biggest bed from the Doll House, with white petal sheets, and a thick red leaf rug beside it.

There stood another red chair, with half a nut-shell for a foot-stool.

And there, on a clump of fern, were neatly hung Mrs. Doll's pink silk ball-gown, lace-edged petticoat and drawers, and Mr. Doll's evening clothes!

"It *must* have been Father!" Annabel cried. "Maybe he's in the next room. Look, William! A bathroom!"

There was a white flower-cup, big enough for a doll's bathtub, filled with fresh water; there was a scrap of cocoanut husk for a bath-mat; there were petal towels; there was a bit of something for soap.*

* *William found by taking a bite (for he was hungry enough to eat even soap) that this was a bit of banana. When Some One (Some One is what I am calling whoever furnished these rooms, until it is time to tell you the real name) hunted for soap in the jungle, Some One thought banana looked more like it than anything else did.*

"So this is our new house!" cried Annabel. "William, you are wonderful! You brought us right to it!"

William wanted to be wonderful, but he had to be honest.

"No, Annabel, our new house is in a coral cave by the sea. I don't know where we are!"

"But Mother and Father must be here! There are their clothes!"

"Their clothes were stolen."

And he thought: "This must be the Robbers' Den!" But he didn't tell Annabel, for fear of frightening her.

No one was there, not even a robber.

"We'd better go on."

"We can't, William. Finny says he's too tired and sleepy and hungry."

And it was getting dark.

"We'll stay here till tomorrow, then," William said. He told himself he wouldn't go to sleep, but watch for the robbers all night, and fight them if they came back to their den.

So he brought out the other red chair, and they had supper on the toadstool. Then Annabel put Finny in the bathtub—that seemed the best place for a fish—and went to bed, while William lay down just inside the door, to wait for robbers.

Before you read this, they were so fast asleep they did not hear some one crying excitedly:

"My dear! Come quickly! Hurry! Run as fast as you can! Just *see* what I've found!"

Chapter Forty-Three

THE DANCE IN THE MOONLIGHT

"My dear! Come quickly! Hurry! Run as fast as you can! Just *see* what I've found!" cried Mr. Doll, excitedly.

Mrs. Doll came quickly, hurried, ran as fast as she could, and saw the two red chairs from the Doll House, on each side of the toadstool, which by this time had grown so tall that it was more like a garden umbrella than a table.

"Did you ever?"

"No, I never!"

"There's something on top of the toadstool, but I'll have to climb up on a chair to see what."

"Wait, wait, my dear!" Mrs. Doll spread a leaf on the seat of the chair. Then Mr. Doll climbed up, stood on tiptoe, and cried:

"Wonders will never cease! Here is the Doll House cream-jug, with a dew-drop in it!"

"Here is a cave! Oh, my dear! It must be the Robbers' Den!"

Mr. Doll crept to the door of the cave, and peeped in.

The moon had risen, and by its light he saw some one lying just inside.

mr. Doll.

Mr. Doll stood on tip-toe.

"Hold up your hands, or I'll fire!" he shouted.
William jumped up, and flew at Mr. Doll so hard that

they both tumbled down, and the dew-drop jumped out of the cream-jug.

You see, Mr. Doll thought William was a robber, and William thought Mr. Doll was a robber, so they were both brave, I think. Don't you?

Imagine their excitement and joy!

After the first few minutes of everyone talking at once, Mr. Doll said:

"We'll spend the night here, and in the morning we three will start out once more to look for Annabel."

"Oh, I wouldn't bother," said William, pretending to be very indifferent.

"Why, *Will*iam! I thought you were so anxious to find your poor little sister!"

At that moment Annabel, with Finny in her arms, came out of the cave. She thought the noise meant robbers, and she didn't want to miss anything.

I don't believe four little dolls have ever been happier.

At last Mrs. Doll got them to bed, after she had made Mr. Doll bring in the red chairs and the cream-jug. William and Annabel fell asleep again on soft cots of leaves. But Mrs. Doll was wakeful. Now that her children were found, she longed to be home again.

"I wish I were in my own bed," she sighed.

"You are in your own bed, my dear."

"I mean in my own house."

"But the House is full of water."

"I mean in our seaside cottage, of course. I don't like visiting strange robbers."

And then she said suddenly:

"What do you suppose they have done with *my wig?"*

She slept at last, and only Mr. Doll lay awake. He never fell asleep as quickly as the others, for he had no weights in his head, to close his eyelids as soon as he lay down.

What was that? Boom-*boom*—boom-*boom*—boom-*boom!*

A drum was beating in the jungle. He had to see what was happening.

He crept out of bed, and through the web a spider had spun across the doorway.

Boom-*boom*—boom-*boom*—boom-*boom*, called the drum, and over the ground and up in the trees Mr. Doll could hear the light footsteps and hidden rustlings of those who were answering it.

The jungle was filled with the beautiful light of the moon, so bright that the white toadstools glistened, and the ferns printed black shadows on them. Mr. Doll followed the sound to a clearing. There perched a toucan, drumming away on a hollow tree. Boom-*boom*—boom-*boom!*

And there crouched a circle of queer little figures. Some sat on their tails as if they were camp stools, one lay on his back, holding his foot. Up in a tree, two huddled close together, their tails loosely entwined. On another, a mother tenderly held her baby to her breast. Mr. Doll could see they were waiting for something.

"Monkeys!" he whispered.

The light of the moon grew brighter, big fireflies shone.

Then some one came out from the shadows.

"Dinah!" gasped Mr. Doll.

There was a quick, angry chatter from the monkeys, as if they were telling him to be quiet.

The little black doll had on nothing but her blue bead ear-rings, a wreath of red and yellow flowers around her neck, and something on her head that shone like pale gold in the moonlight.

It was—it couldn't be—yes, it was ——

Mrs. Doll's wig!

She walked to the middle of the clearing, and began

The Toucan Stopped Drumming

dancing to the toucan's drumming. Slowly at first, then faster and faster. The moonlight caught on the whites of her eyes, the blue ear-rings, the wig, and the wreath that leaped up and down on her neck. All the rest was ink-black, and her long ink-black shadow danced with her as if it were tied to her heels.

"Dinah!" shouted Mr. Doll.

At the sound of his voice Dinah stopped dancing, the toucan stopped drumming. The jungle sucked in the monkeys. Not one was left.

"Mr. Doll!" cried Dinah, snatching off the wig. "Is Mrs. Doll here?"

"She's asleep, in a furnished cave we found."

"Yes, sir. That's my cave. I furnished it, but my friends brought the furniture ——"

"Your friends?"

"Yes, sir, the monkeys. A monkey stole me, too, out of a tree. But they like me now, and I like them. They think I'm a sort of queen. I've been very happy with them. Mr. Doll, sir ——"

"Yes, Dinah?"

"I'm ashamed of wearing Mrs. Doll's wig. I always wanted to, but I haven't really enjoyed it. It just makes me feel blacker."

"Say no more about it!" said Mr. Doll, kindly.

"Thank you, sir. I won't."

"Neither will I."

"I'll come and get breakfast for you tomorrow morning, sir, and tell you about everything."

Chapter Forty-Four

THE PROCESSION THROUGH THE TREE-TOPS

The next morning when Mr. and Mrs. Doll, Annabel, William, and Finny came out from the cave, there was Dinah in a red flower dress, walking up from the River with the cream-jug full of water balanced on her head. A new toadstool table was set with a delicious breakfast in nutshells. The morning air was full of fragrance and bird-calls, sunshine poured through banana leaves as if they had been green glass, and filled the cup of every flower, so the petals were like coloured light, with the veins showing dark.

Mrs. Doll and Annabel wore fresh white flowers, Mr. Doll and William fresh green leaves. And Mrs. Doll had on her wig, and thanked Dinah very much for having found it.

While they ate, Dinah told her story.

You know about the fish. You know how the sea gull picked her up and dropped her. I'm afraid Dinah gave them to understand that she had told him to do so, and he had meekly obeyed her.

"Dinah is growing boastful," thought Mrs. Doll, but Mr. Doll said:

"Yes, I can understand that very well, for when I was out in my canoe —— By the way, I was sorry you couldn't wait for me that day, Dinah!"

"So was I, sir, but thank you just the same for coming."

"When I was in my canoe, a black-and-yellow fish a good deal larger than a whale was rather troublesome, and I simply looked straight at her and ordered her off, and she went. Courage! That's all that is needed!"

"I can understand, too!" cried William. "When I was down in the Crab's hole I ——"

"That will do, William dear," said Mrs. Doll. "We must never boast!"

You already know how Dinah walked on the branch, and how the chameleons came. Dinah said of course it was silly of the chameleons, but they thought her singing was so beautiful that they had blown up and nearly burst.

"Dinah is growing *very* boastful," thought Mrs. Doll, and Mr. Doll thought he would like to sing his canoe song to the chameleons. Perhaps he had better not, though. He couldn't help feeling that such a very beautiful song might make them really burst.

"And then a hand came out of the leaves," said Dinah, stretching out her hand toward Mrs. Doll. "And *grabbed* me!"

Mrs. Doll was so startled that she screamed and pushed back hard against the toadstool, which broke softly and let her down on the ground.

"It was a monkey!" said Dinah. "And what do you think he had on?"

"My wig!" cried Mrs. Doll.

Dinah gave a little jump. Then she said:

"No, ma'am; your lace-edged drawers. He didn't know how to wear them. He had one arm through a leg. I don't believe jungle monkeys are used to wearing lace-edged drawers."

"So that's where the clothes from the clothes-line went!" exclaimed Mrs. Doll.

"Yes, ma'am, the monkeys brought all the clothes and the furniture. Mr. Doll's evening clothes were faded and stained, so I dyed them black by washing them with paw-paw leaves ———"

"How did you know about that?"

"I seemed to remember, somehow. And I put the other

things into the cave to keep them nice until I found you. I found what would do for sheets and towels and soap ———"

A Monkey Tries on the Lace-Edged Drawers.

"*Savon de Banan,*" said Mrs. Doll.
"Ma'am?"

"I was only saying Banana Soap in French, Dinah," Mrs. Doll explained.*

"Yes'm. Well, I'll make the monkeys carry your things back, and carry us, too. When they brought me here, one of the baby monkeys had a fever, and I cured it with wet leaf compresses. They're very grateful; they do whatever I tell them. They think I'm sort of a queen."

"Dinah is growing VERY boastful!" thought Mrs. Doll.

But it was comforting to know they would be carried home, instead of having the long hard journey on foot.

After breakfast the procession started through the tree-tops.

First a monkey carrying the furniture, crated in a broken cocoanut shell tied together with strips of palm.

Then a monkey carrying the clothes, packed in an empty bird's-nest.

Then a monkey carrying Mr. Doll in a new sun-helmet, then one with Mrs. Doll in her wig, then one with William, one with Annabel, and one with Dinah.

Then a very small monkey carrying Finny.

I'm afraid Mrs. Doll was showing off. She had learned a little French, and a song called "Au Clair de la Lune," from a French doll in the Toy Shop.

Then a lot of monkeys carrying nothing, but coming along for fun.

Soon, for the monkeys were quick, and knew all the short cuts, they had swished through leaves and lizards (who whisked out of the way) and orchids and ferns, and past a macaw that Mr. and Mrs. Doll bowed to politely, though I'm not sure whether she was their friend or not, and were down on the beach, with Baby waving his arms, and old Crab and small Crab waving their claws, and the caretaker Angel Fish swimming around in circles, and were all together again!

Chapter Forty-Five

HOME LIFE ON FLOATING ISLAND

"Now, ma'am, we'll set the House straight!" said Dinah.

"But how?"

"Oh, I'll get the monkeys to do it."

"Dinah has grown so grand, she thinks she can make those monkeys do anything!" Mrs. Doll said to Mr. Doll.

"And so she can, my dear!" Mr. Doll answered.

First they unpacked the cocoanut shell, then used it as a scoop to scoop out the Angel Fish. They all thanked him for taking such good care of the House, and Mrs. Doll said she would be glad to recommend him, if he ever thought of looking for another position. Then, with a good-bye whisk of his tail, the Angel Fish swam out to sea.

Next, the Dolls and the monkeys made ropes with which to pull up the Doll House. They braided roots and strips of cocoanut palm, and the monkeys kept braiding their tails in, and having to be unbraided by Mrs. Doll and Dinah. But at last the ropes were finished, and fastened to the House. The Dolls and the monkeys

PULLED

and *up* came the Doll House, with a waterfall cascading from every room.

The
Caretaker Angel-Fish

Mr. Doll wanted to make a speech of thanks to the monkeys, but Mrs. Doll and Dinah had already started house-cleaning, William had taken Annabel to show her the historical spots of the beach* and see if they could find a shrimp, the monkeys were playing Last Tag up and down the cocoanut palm that leaned over the sand, and there was no one to listen but Baby and the Crabs, who had done nothing but wave. He was beginning a little speech to them, when Mrs. Doll called:

"My dear! Come and help us spread the carpets to dry in the sun!"

They carried in the furniture from the Cave in the Roots and Coral Cottage, and some of the prettiest shells and bits of coral. But Dinah kept a few things in Coral Cottage, and used it for her kitchen. She said it was as good as a soap-box. The empty bird's-nest she turned into a clothes-hamper.

Life in the Doll House began again, almost as peacefully as if they were still in the Toy Shop.

Mr. Doll and William thought:

"What is the use of being cast up on a desert island if you don't lead a wild life?"

But Mrs. Doll had other ideas.

* *Mr. Doll's Waterfall, Look-Out Hill, Old Crab's Pool (by the easy way under the Rocks) and the Circle of Rocks. They just looked down into that.*

Every morning she had a talk with Dinah in Coral Cottage Kitchen, and said: "Well, Dinah, I think an air leg of mutton and air cauliflower would be nice today, with Pudding afterwards"; or, "We'll have Finny for lunch, and plenty of air spinach for the children, please." You remember that the Dolls often pretended to eat Pudding, Chicky, Lobby, and Finny, although they never really did. Pudding, Chicky, Lobby, and Finny loved to be chosen for lunch or supper, and could hardly wait for their turns to come.

Then Mrs. Doll would call:

"Now, chickabiddies!"

That meant William and Annabel must come for their lessons; doing sums with shells, practising writing on the sand, and telling what Floating Island was bounded by.

Mrs. Doll had a good deal of trouble with the monkeys. She thought they spent too much time around the Doll House and Coral Cottage.

"Dinah has *far* too much company!" she said to Mr. Doll.

One trouble was that the monkeys admired Mrs. Doll so much that they couldn't leave her alone. She would be sitting at the piano, playing "The Waltz of the Dolls," and the first thing she knew, she would be upside down in a

Mr. Doll Tries to Teach the Parrots to Speak Pieces

monkey's hand, and the monkey would be gazing at her with the greatest wonder and interest. One carried her to the top of the tree with the yellow and crimson flowers, and frightened her dreadfully by holding her by the foot while he swung from a branch. Of course he thought he was giving her a treat.

She talked to them severely, and so did Dinah, but she seemed so wonderful to them, they couldn't let her alone. They tried to do whatever she did—play the piano, or hold up their tails as she held up the train of a leaf dress.

One very small monkey was always taking things that belonged to her, for no one had ever told him that was wrong, and he had always taken what he liked in the jungle; fruit, or nuts. He found her ball-gown (which of course she didn't wear for every day on the beach) carried it up the cocoanut palm, and put it on. But he didn't know how to wear it. He pulled it on his head, like a cap, with the train going down in a point on his back. And when Mrs. Doll called to him: "Please bring me my dress *at once!*" he threw down a cocoanut for a present, and nearly smashed her.

"Such neighbours!" sighed Mrs. Doll.

But she knew they behaved that way only because they didn't know any better. And she felt grateful to them for all their help in carrying the family home through the jungle, in pulling up the Doll House, and in bringing presents of fruit and nuts. So, as she wanted to do something for them, she gave them dancing-lessons.

The trouble about teaching the monkeys to dance was that they would turn somersaults, or run up a tree and swing by their tails, or stop to scratch their heads, in the middle of every waltz, and if you have been to dancing-school, you know, while it may be fun, that isn't the way to do it.

She did something else for the monkeys. She made the Doll House carpets into trousers for as many as she could. Dinah's especial friend, the one who stole her from the branch, had green trousers with a pattern of red rosebuds, made from the parlour carpet.

Since the Doll House floors looked bare, Mr. Doll sanded them in pretty patterns. On one floor he made sand ripples, as if waves had marked them; on one, whirly ferns; on one, a pinwheel; and on the parlour floor, a big rose.

Mr. Doll gave lessons, too. He had a class of parrots, and tried to teach them to speak pieces.

But it wasn't all lessons on Floating Island. They only took an hour or two every morning, and then the children and Mr. Doll could bathe in the sea, or look at the hermit crabs, that crept into empty mollusk shells and carried them about for houses, their claws sticking out like bunches of empty glove-fingers.

Or Mr. Doll would lead William and Annabel up the cocoanut palm, and then they would toboggan down. That was fun!

Or they would go to their favourite place. Under the waterfall, really under, between rocks and leaping water, where it was like being in a sliding, curved glass house.

Sometimes they would explore the jungle with Dinah, who knew her way about as if she had been born there. She showed them so many strange things. Pitcher-plants full of water, silver ferns that would print patterns on you if you pressed them against yourself. The silver patterns showed better on Dinah than on the children.

Sometimes, when the moon was full, she would slip off by herself into the jungle. Mr. Doll wondered if she was dancing again; and Mrs. Doll would say, sadly:

"We have really lost her, this time!"

But Dinah always came back.

Chapter Forty-Six

MR. DOLL'S BOOK

"My dear, there is something I want you to do," Mrs. Doll said to Mr. Doll, one morning. "We have had strange adventures on Floating Island."

"Yes, my dear."

"Not many dolls have seen the things we have seen."

"No, my dear."

"So I want you to write a book about them!"

"My dear! *I* couldn't write a book!"

"Well, maybe you couldn't."

"But I can try," said Mr. Doll, hastily. He really liked the idea, but he thought he ought to be modest to begin with.

So a quiet cave down the beach was fitted up for a study by Mrs. Doll who wrote on the sand outside it:

"DO NOT DISTURB!"

Mr. Doll's ink was the juice of crushed purple flowers, and his quill pen was made from a humming-bird's feather.

This is the way he went to work to write his book.

Mr. Doll at Work on His Book

He took a swim every morning, to clear his brain.
Then a sun-bath.
Then a brisk walk along the beach.
Then he sat by the waterfall to collect his thoughts.

Mr. Doll begins his Book

Then a nap, because his brain was tired.
Then a swim, to wake himself up.
Then it was supper-time.
Then he watched the stars.
And then it was bedtime.

This went on until Mrs. Doll said:

"My dear, that isn't the way to write a book! Go into your study after breakfast, and write. Dinah will bring you your lunch on a tray, and you'd better not work later than five o'clock every day."

William and Annabel were to keep crabs, sea gulls, and monkeys from looking in. But they looked in themselves, very often, to say:

"How are you getting on, Father?"

So Mr. Doll, not very eagerly, tried Mrs. Doll's way.

And here is what he had finished by the end of a week:

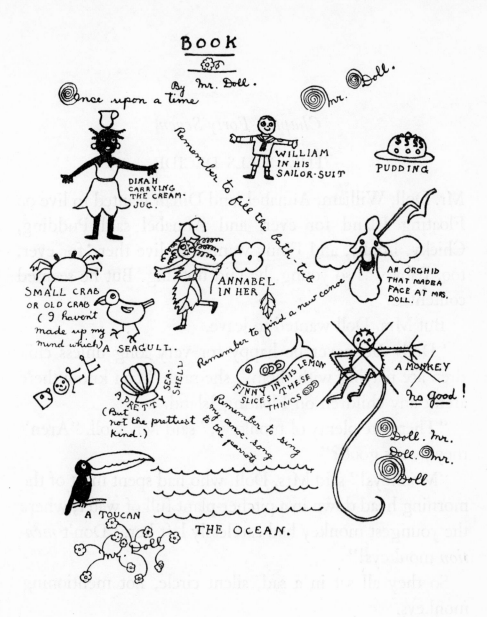

BOOK

By Mr. Doll.

Once upon a time

Mr. Doll.

Mr. Doll.

DINAH CARRYING THE CREAM-JUG.

WILLIAM IN HIS SAILOR-SUIT

PUDDING

Remember to fill the bath-tub

SMALL CRAB OR OLD CRAB (I haven't made up my mind which)

A SEAGULL.

ANNABEL IN HER

AN ORCHID THAT MADE A FACE AT MRS. DOLL.

A PRETTY SEA-SHELL (But not the prettiest kind.)

Remember to find a new canoe

FINNY IN HIS LEMON SLICES. THESE THINGS

Remember to sing my canoe-song to the parrot

A MONKEY

no good!

Doll. Mr. Doll. Mr. Doll.

A TOUCAN

THE OCEAN.

Mr. Doll.

Chapter Forty-Seven

THE DOLLS DECIDE

Mr. Doll, William, Annabel, and Dinah wanted to live on Floating Island for ever, and Annabel said Pudding, Chicky, Lobby, and Finny wanted to live there for ever, too. Baby was so young, he said nothing. But he seemed contented.

But Mrs. Doll wanted to leave.

"Dolls can never be happy for very long unless children are playing with them," she said. "You know there aren't any children on Floating Island."

"There are plenty of monkeys," said Mr. Doll. "Aren't they just as good?"

"Monkeys!" said Mrs. Doll, who had spent most of the morning head down in a pitcher-plant full of water, where the youngest monkey had carelessly left her. "Don't *mention* monkeys!"

So they all sat in a sad, silent circle, not mentioning monkeys.

"Dolls need children, and children need dolls," said Mrs. Doll. "Don't you remember the stories Peony Sealingwax used to tell us in the Toy Shop? Don't you remember how we used to long to go to children, and have splendid times like hers?"*

* *Peony Sealingwax was a doll-house doll who belonged to a little girl named Nancy, or else Nancy belonged to her, the Dolls weren't sure which. Nancy had taken Peony into her bath too often, so that Peony had become unstrung and had been sent to the Toy Shop to be put together again.*

She had become a great friend of the Dolls, and used to tell them about her family; Mr. and Mrs. Sealingwax, her sister, Pansy Sealingwax, her brothers, Lionel and Walnut Sealingwax, and their cook, who was glass, wore a handkerchief dress, and had a cork head with her face drawn on in ink. The Cook's name was Katie Pillbottle. Dinah liked hearing about her best of all.

Nancy and her little brother David played with the Sealingwax family all the time, Peony said, and they had such fun! The Sealingwax doll house wasn't as grand as our Doll's Doll House. It was quite old and shabby, and some of the furniture was broken, but Peony loved it. When Mrs. Doll showed her the beauties of the Doll House, Peony said,

"There's no place like home," more often than Mrs. Doll thought was polite.

The Sealingwaxes had a pink wax cockatoo in a gilt cage. He had melted a little, but not too badly. They had a china cup without a handle for a bathtub. When Mrs. Doll showed Peony the tin tub in the Doll House, Peony said, "We have a porcelain *tub,* at home!" David had made a bed for Peony by gluing blue velvet on a cigar-box. There was a chest of drawers made of match-boxes, three glued together. The drawers would really pull out and hold things—bird-seed, Peony's hat, or a cherry-stone.

When Nancy and David had their supper, the Sealing-wax family often sat on the table, in the pleasant steam rising from bowls of milk-toast, and had it with them. Katie Pillbottle always had most, because Nancy and David would take out her cork head and put a little cambric tea or a rasp-berry inside her.

Sometimes the Sealingwax family went for rides in a shoe, hitched to Neddy, the plaster donkey. He had lost one leg and had to be propped up with a book or a building-block, but he never complained of his loss, and they all loved him. His head would come off, like Katie Pillbottle's. Some-times it was mislaid, but Neddy no more minded losing his head than losing his leg. Sometimes his neck looked very long and as if he were wearing a high white cardboard collar. Sometimes his head would be looking straight up at the sky, or a few bits of grass and clover would stick out of the crack around his neck, after Nancy and David had been feeding him.

Sometimes Nancy and David took the Sealingwax family for rides in pockets, or in the fronts of their sailor blouses.

Sometimes they were so kind as to allow one of the Sealingwaxes to stay out in the garden all night. Peony told our Dolls of a night she had spent in the vegetable garden, in a forest of asparagus fern, watching by moonlight the beautiful crystals of dew.

And, on other nights, in the playroom, when the children were asleep, and moonlight lay like squares of snow on the carpet, a small mouse with long whiskers, an intimate friend of the Sealingwax family, often visited them.

Every winter a beautiful tree with a delicious fragrance grew up in the playroom, Peony said. Nancy and David called it the Christmas tree. One day it would be there, bare except for its dark green needles ———

"Leaves, I think, dear," Mrs. Doll had corrected her.

Peony was a polite little doll, but she was sure they were needles. Green things on trees out-of-doors were leaves, she *knew, but green things on trees in playrooms were needles. Nancy and David had said so.*

"Were they sharp?" asked Mr. Doll, who had been examining a Toy Shop work-box the night before.

"Very sharp," answered Peony.

"Needles, my dear," Mr. Doll said to Mrs. Doll. "You were telling us—let me see, what were you telling us, Miss Peony Sealingwax?"

Peony said she had been telling them about the tree in the playroom, bare the first day, but always, next morning, full of shining fruit, gold, silver, crimson, and blue, with an angel on the tip-top branch. Sometimes the candles on its boughs would be lighted, and burn until they wept wax tears. Sometimes a candle-flame would scorch a branch, that would give out the best smell in the world.

Then when its needles ——

"Leaves, I still think," said Mrs. Doll. "Go on, Peony dear. We are all so much interested!"

So Peony went on, and told how the tree's needles would begin to drop, and sometimes a shining fruit would fall lightly, and splinter into stars all over the carpet.

At the end of a week the tree would be taken away.

Interesting visitors came to Sealingwax House, Peony said. A gingerbread lady and gentleman, with buttons and

Sometimes They Kindly Allowed Peony to Stay Out All Night

coats and pleasant smiles all marked by white icing, had lived first in the wonderful tree, and, when that was taken away, had moved to Sealingwax House, after Nancy and David had found Herr and Frau Pfefferkuchen were so hard they could only make teeth dents on them. The ginger-

Katie Pillbottle and her friends, Herr and Frau Pfeffer-Kuchen.

bread lady and gentleman had travelled, could tell about storks, and pine forests, and blue cornflowers in fields of yellow wheat, and, besides, could sing, "Ach, du liebe Augustine."

Then there was Aunt Wishbone, who lived in the desk and wiped all the pens on her scalloped flannel petticoats.

Yes, they all remembered Peony Sealingwax, and her stories.

"Children are waiting for us somewhere," said Mrs. Doll. "We must think of that."

Mr. Doll went and sat by himself on the top of Look-Out Hill. William and Annabel took Pudding, went under the waterfall, and sat in their green-and-white house of sliding water until they were covered with beads of spray. They all thought hard.

That evening at supper Mr. Doll said:

Nancy and David often brought her to visit the Sealing-waxes, or took them to visit Aunt Wishbone's desk, with its little wooden rooms and big green-blotter carpet.

Each day was better than the one before, when you lived with children, Peony said. You never could guess what they would do with you next. She had lived in a Toy Shop once, herself, but she wouldn't go back to that for anything. "Of course it is pleasant for a visit, like this," she added. "But not to live in. Too crowded, too many strangers, and no real home life." She pitied our Dolls, because the only children they knew were the ones who came to the Toy Shop, looked at them, and were told by grown-ups, "Mustn't touch!"

"My dear, I have decided you are right about leaving Floating Island. We must go where there are children."

William said:

"Annabel and I think so, too."

And Annabel said:

"Pudding wants to live in a nice dry nursery, because he is getting all green with mould from sea air and waterfall spray."

Chapter Forty-Eight

THE BANQUET

"But how shall we get away?" Mrs. Doll asked.

"We must build a signal fire," said Mr. Doll. "That is what people do when they are cast up on a desert island. They build a fire, and then a ship sees it and rescues them."

"Before we go, I want to give a farewell banquet for all the friends who have been kind to us," Mrs. Doll said.

"Let's give it the night we light our signal fire," said Mr. Doll. "Banquet first, with a Waltz of the Monkeys to follow, then the lighting of the fire! And I will make a speech!"

All of them, even Mrs. Doll, felt so sorry to leave Floating Island that they tried not to give themselves time to think about it. They fell to work, preparing for the banquet and the bonfire.

Mr. Doll and William laid the fire on top of Look-Out Hill, ready for lighting.

There is a tree on Floating Island called the cashew tree. It is full of fruit, like yellow pears, and at the end of each fruit, like a curly tail on a pig, hangs a cashew nut shaped like this comma, only much bigger. Dinah told them the nutshells were so full of oil that they would fizz and blaze when they were lighted, so they put first a big heap of cashew nut shells (saving the nuts for the banquet). On top of these they piled all the driftwood they could carry. They worked for days, Dolls and monkeys, getting a heap that would be big enough.

Mrs. Doll, Dinah, and Annabel worked hard, too. They gathered new shell cups and dishes, and petal napkins. They marked a big square on the sand, for the table, and outlined it with a lace-like edge of tiny snow-white shells. Mrs. Doll planned a beautiful centerpiece of long trails of little scarlet orchids, and William dug in the sand, in the middle of the table, until he came to water. That made a vase to put the stems in. He dug another well, at one of the places, and a moat from it to the sea, so the caretaker Angel Fish could be wet and comfortable if he came back to the banquet. They sent him an invitation written with a sharp stick on seaweed, but I'm afraid it never reached him, for he didn't come.

"Beautiful! beautiful!" cried Mr. Doll, looking at the table. "And what are we going to give our guests to eat?"

"Oh dear!" exclaimed Mrs. Doll. "I never thought of that!"

For, as you know, the Dolls could sit down to a dinner of plaster chicken and plaster pudding, and cups of air, and get up, leaving the chicken and pudding whole, and the air in the cups, feeling they had had a splendid meal.

"There are the cashew nuts," said Mr. Doll.

"They wouldn't begin to go around."

Just then something fell from one of the trees that hung over the sand, and burst at their feet. It was a fruit the size of an orange; purple, with a pink lining, and inside was what looked like melting lumps of snow.*

"Dinner from the sky!" cried Mr. Doll.

"Yes, sir! Yes, ma'am!" said Dinah. "And I know where we can get plenty of other good things to eat! Pomegranates, grenadillas, sweet sops, sour sops, golden apples, mangoes, cherimoyas, come-to-help-us ———"

"How does Dinah know so much?" Mr. Doll asked, admiringly.

"I believe the monkeys tell her!" Mrs. Doll answered.

When the banquet was ready, it really looked beautiful. There were piles of delicious fruit on the snow-white sand.

* It was the fruit called mangosteen.

Custard apples, cream-coloured with dark-green patterns; puffy orange tangerines; star apples; and the rest of the

Mr. Doll.

Baby.

I meant to draw the whole Banquet, but Mrs.
Doll thought it was time I drew a picture of
Baby, so here he is, waiting to be dressed for
the Banquet. Mr. Doll.
But I wanted Baby drawn in his best dress!
Oh, dear! Mrs. Doll.

fruits Dinah had told them about. And there were sweet trumpet-flowers full of honey, for the humming-birds.

The only trouble was to keep the guests away until the Dolls were ready to receive them. Already the trees were full of birds and monkeys, the sand was covered with sea gulls and crabs. Dinah had to stand by the table shouting, "Shoo! Shoo!" while Mr. Doll hurried into his evening clothes, and Mrs. Doll, already wearing her ball-gown, dressed William in his sailor-suit, and Baby in his white dress. Since Annabel had lost her clothes, she had to wear a white flower. But it had a scalloped edge and looked like silk.

Pudding, Finny, Chicky, and Lobby, each with a tiny flower on top of him, were to sit at the table like the rest of the family, instead of being part of the dinner, as usual.

Mrs. Doll told everyone where to sit, but her guests paid no attention. The crabs and the sea gulls walked over the table, the parrots and parakeets and macaws stayed up in the branches. However, they all seemed happy, so she stopped worrying about it.

A sloth came to the party. They had never seen him before, and he had done nothing for them, but he looked so old, they were glad to have him there enjoying himself. He had a goblin face and green fur,* and he hung head

* *The sloth's fur isn't really green, but is so covered with tiny green creatures called parasites that it looks so. The*

down among the white-lined green leaves of a trumpet-
tree, too lazy to do anything but eat the young pink shoots
very—very—slow—ly ——

A toucan sat in the trumpet-tree, too, eating his dinner.
The Dolls didn't want to be rude, but they couldn't help
staring each time he swallowed a berry, for they could
watch it go all the way down his throat.

Hundreds of small butterflies crowded so close together
on a loop of vine that Mrs. Doll thought they were flowers, until they flew up and away, then down in a circle on
the sand, where one of the monkeys had spilled the juice
of a fruit. They were like a yellow garland with petals that
kept flying up, hovering, dancing in the air, settling again.
Then they would fold their wings close, and the breeze
would slant them all one way, like tiny sailboats.

Dinah had to keep pulling the monkeys off the table by

*sloth doesn't at all mind the parasites living on him. At least,
he has never said that he minded.*

*The sloth spends all his life hanging head down. Some-
times he crawls slowly along the branches, always hanging
from the under side.*

*The baby sloths cling tight to their mothers. They have
to do the holding on, for the mothers use arms and legs to
crawl along the branches.*

their tails, and Mr. Doll sometimes said, "Shoo!" to the sea
gulls. But he said it so pleasantly that they didn't feel badly,
or, indeed, pay any attention.

The Dolls tried to enjoy the tropical fruit, for they felt it
would be more polite to eat what their guests were eating
than just eat air, as usual. They shared a fruit with a spongy
outside, full of yellow strings, and a middle like soft soap.

"This is very—well, interesting, my dear," said Mr.
Doll, smiling pleasantly, and trying to suck in long yellow
threads that hung out of his mouth like a Chinese man-
darin's moustache. "It tastes of boiled custard and soap, a
little apple-sauce, and a good deal of turpentine, wouldn't
you say?"

As it grew dark, and the trees began to glow softly with
the green fire of thousands of fireflies, who had kindly
come to light the feast, Mr. Doll rose to make his speech.

"Ladies and Gentlemen! Friends!"

The monkeys chattered, the parrots Mr. Doll had been
teaching began to call: "Anna-*bel!* Will-*yum!* Ba-*bee!*"
The crabs bubbled and ticked. Only a few rude sea gulls
flew away.

"We of the Doll House wish to thank you for all the
kindness you have shown us since we came to live on Float-

ing Island. We will never forget you, and we hope you will remember us when we are far away!"

Then, because they all felt like crying, Mrs. Doll quickly began to play "The Waltz of the Dolls," and Mr. Doll, William, Annabel, Dinah, and the monkeys danced by the light of the rising moon.

When the waltz was over they all climbed Look-Out Hill, where the pile of driftwood and nutshells waited. The pointed leaves of the palms were ink-black against a sky where heat lightning quivered and the moon hung full and red. Below them they heard the soft thunder of breaking waves.

"Shall I light the fire?" Mr. Doll whispered.

For a moment, Mrs. Doll wanted to cry: "No! Don't light it! Let us stay on Floating Island always!"

But she said:

"Light the fire!"

Chapter Forty-Nine

THE SIGNAL FIRE

Mr. Doll rubbed two dry sticks together, faster and faster, until sparks flew out and fell among the cashew nut shells. A thin tongue of flame licked up through the driftwood —another—then the pile caught, and the fire went crackling and roaring up towards the moon.

The flames painted waves and foam and waterfall. The colours of the sea that had soaked into the driftwood came out again in leaping blue and green. The little figures of Dolls and monkeys were black against the blaze; animals came out of the jungle to see it, their green eyes gleamed from the shadows.

The Dolls piled on more wood—more. The monkeys helped. They had to be stopped from putting on the Doll House furniture. The moon sank into the sea, but nobody noticed, the fire was so bright.

Not even Mrs. Doll thought of saying:

"Bedtime, children!"

What was that, far out at sea? A rocket shot into the sky and burst in a shower of coloured stars.

"A ship has seen our signal!" cried Mr. Doll.

"We must hurry down to the House, and be ready!" Mrs. Doll answered.

Dinah Persuades a monkey not to put a Chair on the Bonfire.

They ran and rolled down Look-Out Hill. A monkey carried the sideboard from Coral Kitchen to the Doll House dining-room, and Lobby, Chicky, Finny, and Pudding were put on it. Baby was put in his crib, William and Annabel went to the nursery, Mr. and Mrs. Doll waited in the parlour.

"But where is Dinah?"

Dinah came slowly into the parlour. She had taken off the plaid dress she had worn all evening, and put on a red flower again.

"Mr. and Mrs. Doll, excuse me, please, but I'm not going with you. I'm going to stay on Floating Island."

"But *Dinah!* Don't you like us any more?"

"Yes, ma'am, I love every one of you, and I always will!" cried Dinah, bursting into tears. "But I feel as if this was home, and I have to stay."

"Think how lonely you'll be, all by yourself here!"

"I'll never be lonely where there are monkeys!"

Mrs. Doll talked in vain. Dinah was sad at parting from them, she would always love them, and she wanted to give Mrs. Doll and Annabel her blue bead ear-rings. But she wouldn't, she couldn't, leave Floating Island.

Mr. Doll envied her.

William, looking out of the nursery window, called: "A boat full of sailors!"

Dinah ran out of the Doll House. William and Annabel pressed to the window, watching, Mrs. Doll leaned against the piano, Mr. Doll against a red chair, as if they had never gone through the jungle, or bathed in the sea, as if they had never moved.

Chapter Fifty

THE SHOOTING STAR

The sailors who answered the beacon fire hunted, shouting, up and down the beach, and even made their way into the jungle.

But they found only a Doll House and a family of Dolls.

One sailor always said that he had seen a monkey wearing little green trousers sprinkled with red rosebuds, running up a tree. But the others never believed him. They said he had been drinking too much rum, which hurt his feelings dreadfully.*

The Dolls grew very fond of this sailor, whose name was Joe. The others in the lifeboat were named Herman the German, One-Eye, Tony, Fat, Mike the Roarer, and Charlie, a homesick little cabin-boy, who was making his first trip.

Later on, Charlie sometimes played with the Dolls and the Doll House, when no one was looking. He didn't know how to play very well. He would just prop Mrs. Doll against

Since they could find nothing else, they put the Doll House into their life-boat, and rowed back to their ship in the rosy sunrise.

mr. Doll.

One Sailor saw a monkey wearing Trousers.

a chair, or move Pudding from sideboard to table. But they were a great comfort to him.

The Dolls, lying on their backs in the Doll House, looked up at the sailors, very much interested. The one nearest them had a full-rigged sailing-ship at sea tattooed on his chest in red and blue. The waves seemed to move, the sails to swell, as he rowed.

Now the life-boat was bobbing up and down under the ship. The Dolls could see the netted reflections of waves moving on her bow, and read her name, *The Shooting Star*. They saw faces looking down, like a row of pink and brown moons, and heard somebody call:

"What did you find?"

The sailor with the ship on his chest shouted back:

"Only a doll house!"

The House was lifted on board, and the Dolls caught one last glimpse of Floating Island, with its foam and flowers, and the white smoke where their signal fire had burned, like a handkerchief waving good-bye.

Chapter Fifty-One

WHERE ARE THEY NOW?

What has become of the Doll House and the Dolls?

I don't know what port *The Shooting Star* was bound for. I don't know who is playing with the Dolls and the Doll House now.

Perhaps they are in your nursery. Look and see if you think so.

Has your Doll House a pointed roof and two surprised-looking chimneys?

Mrs. Doll may have lost her wig again, or she may have a new one. But has your Mrs. Doll bright pink cheeks? Does she stand up as straight as a poker?

Has your Mr. Doll bright pink cheeks, a pleasant smile, and a crack in his black china hair?

Can your little boy and girl (for I don't know what names you have given to William and Annabel) bend at the joints and turn their heads?

Does your Baby kick his legs and hold up pink hands?

And have your Dolls surprised-looking eyebrows, as if they were remembering strange adventures?

No use asking about Dinah. I know she is still with the monkeys. But have you Pudding or Lobby or Chicky or Finny? Or a blue tin bathtub? Or a cream-jug that looks like silver but is easily bent?

Your dolls are yours to keep, always, but I wonder if they are the Dolls I used to know.

If you think they are, will you tell me?

The Farewell Speech
Self-Portrait by
Mr. Doll.

And have your Dolls surprised-looking eyebrows, as if
    they were remembering strange adventures?
No use asking about Dinah, I know she is still with the
monkeys, but have you Pudding or Lobby or Chicky or
Finny? Or a blue tin bathtub? Or a cream-jug that looks
    like silver but is easily bent?
    Your dolls are yours to keep, always, but I wonder if
    they are the Dolls I used to know.
    If you think they are, will you tell me?